PASSPORT TO DEATH

Also By Yigal Zur

Death in Shangri-La

PASSPORT TO DEATH

A DOTAN NAOR THRILLER

YIGAL ZUR

Translated from Hebrew by Sara Kitai

OCEANVIEW PUBLISHING

SARASOTA, FLORIDA

Published in the United States by Oceanview Publishing, 2019

First published in Israel (Hebrew) by Kinneret, Zmora-Bitan, Dvir Publishing House Ltd., 2011

ISBN 978-1-60809-364-9

Cover Design by Christian Fuenfhausen

Translated from Hebrew by Sara Kitai

This translation published in the United States of America by Oceanview Publishing, Sarasota, Florida

www.oceanviewpub.com

10 9 8 7 6 5 4 3 2 1

PRINTED IN THE UNITED STATES OF AMERICA

FOR KARIN

Amazing artist, great wife—for all the good times

ACKNOWLEDGMENTS

To Murray Weiss, my agent, for your wise counsel and commitment. To Gregory Bekerman, for your help in Russian-Israeli slang. To Felix Khachaturian for your vision. To Sara & Ammnon Grushka for putting up with me and my stories for so many years. Thanks to Sara Kitai for the amazing translation. To all the team at Oceanview: Pat & Bob Gussin, Lee Randall, and Autumn Beckett—thank you for welcoming me with open arms. To my beloved sons, Kay & Nitai, for the light. And to my wonderful wife, Karin, for unlimited love.

PASSPORT TO DEATH

CHAPTER ONE

I WAS AT my regular corner table in the back of the coffee house in Masaryk Square, far from the bright light streaming in through the south-facing window, sitting with my back to the wall as usual. I was leisurely sipping an espresso as I leafed through the morning paper, waiting for Mira to finish her shopping and come pick me up. Then my cell phone came to life in the pocket of my jeans.

It was my partner, Shai. "Dotan," he said, "we've got a case. This time it's Bangkok. A missing woman." Silence.

"That's it?" I grumbled. "You're really drowning me in info." I already missed the ease I was feeling before I answered the phone. I took another sip. I always liked the coffee here, but this time it was particularly good, a strong intriguing blend.

"Listen up," Shai said with obvious impatience. "Her name is Sigal Bardon, twenty-six. I'm getting the details now. You ought to get down here right away." Lately my conversations with Shai were as brief as possible, and I don't even want to talk about the taste they left in my mouth. Our partnership was going south. For a lot of reasons.

I got up reluctantly, to put it mildly.

"You didn't finish your coffee," Nora, the longtime waitress, said. She'd started working here years ago when she was a student, studying art or cinema or something like that, and never left. I'd also started having my coffee here years ago, and I was still here too.

"What is it?" she asked. "A case?"

I flashed her a smile. It's easy to smile at Nora. Slender body, ample perky boobs, flowing red hair. Wherever your looked, figure or face, she was a sight to behold, even though she wasn't a kid anymore. And you could tell she wasn't burdened by a permanent man in her life.

"The coffee—a new blend?" I asked.

This time it was she who smiled as she gave me a thumbs-up. "Should I save some for when you get back?"

I mumbled an answer, left her a generous tip, as usual, and left. The light was almost blinding, the abrasive glare of late spring. The comforting grayish light of a Tel Aviv winter was gone. I hailed a cab. As I settled into the back seat, I remembered to call Mira. "I'm on the way to the office, baby. I'm guessing I'll have to catch the night flight to Bangkok."

"Again? You just got back."

"I'll make it up to you when I get home, sweetie."

"Should I tell you how many times I've heard that?"

I heard her sigh as she disconnected. We both knew it was a lost cause—us, I mean, not the case.

"Wow," the cabbie started badgering me as soon as I finished the call. "What I wouldn't give to go to Bangkok again." I could see his cloudy eyes in the mirror. You can't avoid those kibitzers. He'd been to Bangkok once, and now I would have to hear about it the whole ride. "I had such a great time, you wouldn't believe it," he went on. "I'd chop off a finger to get on a plane right now."

I tuned him out. I pictured the body of a young woman lying naked on the bed or floor of a room in a no-star hotel. I could see the screaming headlines in tomorrow's papers: "26-Year-Old Israeli Woman Found Dead in Bangkok Guesthouse: Autopsy Reveals Heart Failure Following Lethal Combination of Alcohol and Drugs."

Drugs. It wouldn't be just any drug. It would be heroin, white magic, Bangkok gold. Throw in alcohol and you get vomiting, convulsions, sweating. An overdose paralyzes the central nervous system, sending the victim into a deep coma. Death follows quickly, within minutes. One second, you're high, and the next, there's a corpse to get through customs. It happens at least once a week in Bangkok.

* * *

Mira drove me to the airport. She almost had to twist my arm to convince me not to call a cab. "It's our quality time," she sighed, "the drive back and forth to the airport."

Mira. The only person who still cares when I come and go. That too, I guessed, would soon be over. Especially considering the fact that we were already living in separate apartments. A "trial separation" it's called. I'd known a few in the past. Somehow these trials never pan out. Or maybe it's the opposite. They work so well that at least one side isn't in a hurry to get back together. Maybe that's why I'd heard myself calling Mira "baby" and "sweetie" lately.

"What's the story?" she asked on the way.

"A missing woman."

"Dead?"

"Don't know. She hasn't been in touch with her family for over two weeks."

"It's so sad," Mira said, her voice filled with compassion. "It's always the family who suffers in the end."

"This family is well known, well connected," I said, adding, "and filthy rich. They asked us to keep a low profile."

"Pretty?"

"What difference does it make?" I said irritably. "They're all pretty."

I remembered the picture in the file Shai prepared for me. The truth? Sigal Bardon was pretty. Very pretty. But it really didn't make any difference.

Mira kissed me lightly on the cheek. "Take care," she said.

It sounded like goodbye. Maybe it was. But my mind was already someplace else.

* * *

The airport was as busy as always. You see the lines at the duty-free shop and you know that life goes on. No matter what's happening outside, beyond the huge glass windows—intifada, economic crisis, whatever—the price of single malt whiskey has gone up, men are sniffing Cuban cigars, and perfumes are being piled into shopping carts like cartons of milk in the supermarket. I bought a few cartons of Marlboros, which in my experience is the incentive most highly prized by the cops in Thailand. Especially Tom, an old friend of mine. I threw in two bottles of Jameson, one for meetings so I wouldn't have to endure the local whiskey, Mekhong, which mangles the digestive system. The other was for the nights, or more precisely, for the mornings after the nights, those never-ending mornings you spend trying to figure out what the hell happened the night before, where you were, and even more importantly, with whom. That's a pivotal question in Bangkok. It can sometimes be a matter of life and death. So a bottle of Jameson is a good idea. It always comes in handy.

CHAPTER TWO

I HAVE A simple method for dealing with long flights: two whiskeys, neat, before dinner, a Campari and tonic as soon as the airborne waitress makes her way back with the drinks cart, and then red wine to make the gooey mush they call airplane food a little more palatable. Afterwards, I lean my seat back as far as it will go in shitty economy class and close my eyes. I wake up with a dry mouth and a slight headache, which is helpful in its own way; it keeps me from losing my cool in the long line at Immigration after we land.

But it doesn't always work.

As soon as I closed my eyes, someone shook my shoulder.

"Are you asleep?"

The girl in the next seat was smiling, if you can call it a smile when there's a bauble stuck in her tongue and another one glinting at you from what's left of her nose.

"Most definitely," I said.

It didn't do any good. "Want some Coke?" she asked, offering me what was left in her plastic cup, believe it or not. Haven't these youngsters ever heard of infectious diseases? But it was a nice gesture. I curled up in sleeping mode, but she was persistent. Her eyes sparkled—not sparkled, glowed—with a passion to experience life.

"Have you been to Bangkok before?"

I muttered something in reply that could be taken to mean any number of things.

"What are you going for?"

"Business." I hoped I said it blandly enough for her to get the message.

"Awesome! I'm staying in Bangkok for a few days. There's a course in Vipassana at a temple in the Banglamphu district. Some famous master is coming; I can't remember his name. But he's important, like the Dalai Lama. After that I'm going on a trek in Chiang Mai. Then, something like two weeks later, I'm going to the islands, probably to Railay Beach to do some rock climbing. Cool, right?" Whew. She didn't even take a breath in the middle. All staccato. She left me no choice. I asked a passing flight attendant for a whiskey soda, no ice. I knew I didn't have an easy flight ahead of me. The moppet was going to chew my ear off until we landed, and then she'd say "bye" with a see-you-later smile, although that was never going to happen. In any case, I wouldn't be getting any sleep.

Luckily, they began screening a film, Bertolucci's *Little Buddha*. My seatmate slipped out of her shoes and settled herself cross-legged on the seat. Putting on her earphones, she disconnected from me. I thanked merciful Buddha, *Om mani padme hum*, and Bertolucci too, for taking pity on me even if they didn't know it. Then I closed my eyes.

CHAPTER THREE

BANGKOK. I'VE BEEN coming here for twenty years and heard all the contradictory descriptions: squalid, a giant whorehouse; beautiful but too hot. We live in an age where after one week we think we know everything. But the city is all that and much more. It's Bangkok.

I was just taking out my passport when Tom appeared. There are Thais and there are Thais. The ones from the north are paler, the ones from the south are darker. And then there's Tom, the biggest and loudest of them all. He's also the most non-Thai Thai person I've ever met. He says what he thinks. He gave himself the name Tom during a short-lived pointless marriage to an American lady, because his Thai name, like many others, is almost as long as the local name of Bangkok itself, which starts with Krung Thep Mahanakhon. No foreigner can remember the rest. Trying to say Tom's full name makes your jaw hurt, so he sticks with Tom.

"My friend," he said, hugging me, or rather squashing me. Laughing, he led me through Immigration, and then was seized by a coughing fit thanks to all the Marlboros he chain smokes.

"It's been a while," I said.

"Where did you disappear to?"

"Our business is growing."

"Business? Does your buddy still think he's the head of Mossad?" Tom snorted through his broad porcine nose, a snort that accurately described the state of our company.

"*Schmattes*, that's all it is."

How a cop in Thailand learned Yiddish expressions, I haven't the faintest idea. I asked him once and he made a veiled reference to private lessons from a well-known rabbi who was caught in Patpong, Bangkok's red-light district, with his pants down.

"Chabad rabbi?" I'd asked.

"No. Haredi. Highly revered by the ultra-Orthodox in your country. He claimed he was there to buy a Rolex watch. When we leaned on him, he said the local religious authorities and kashrut inspectors weren't reliable, so he'd come to check out the goods himself."

Tom has a phrase for every situation. If you consider a ten-word vocabulary knowing a language, I bet he knows more languages than anyone else.

That's how it is when you work for the Tourist Police in Bangkok. Citizens from every country in the world wind up in Bangkok. And like everyone else on the force, Tom believes that if they're in his city, they're undoubtedly breaking some law. So if he can say "fuck you," "you're screwed," and "show me the money" in their language, a lot of pain and red tape can be avoided before they ever see a jail cell.

Outside the terminal it was drizzling. I've yet to arrive in Bangkok when it wasn't raining. Some people get lucky and it starts raining when they leave, putting them in a nostalgic mood. With me it's the opposite. The rain tells me I just got here and the shit is already flying.

When the driver of the white Toyota squad car caught sight of us at the exit, he hastily opened a wide umbrella. He was a small fellow with a pockmarked face and the gaunt appearance of someone with a multitude of needle marks in his arms. In his case, they were covered in tattoos. Over his brow, the word "Gai" was shaved into his hair.

"This is Gai," Tom said, introducing him. "It means chick." He saw me checking him out and added, "Don't get the wrong idea. He's no baby chick. There's nowhere you can't go if you've got him by your side. When he goes ballistic, he can plow through ten men, easy."

Tom had an amazing talent to surround himself with psychos. Some people are magnets for the fucked up. The thought made me shudder: maybe that's why we'd been friends for so long. On the other hand, maybe the reason our friendship had endured was that we didn't see each other very often. It was the same with the women in my life, except that it worked better with Tom.

"He was apprenticed to a monk in an outlying temple near Ayutthaya," Tom explained as the white Toyota pulled onto the highway that would take us from the airport into the city. "When he was fourteen, he fell in love and left the monastery, but then he found out that the girl was really a ladyboy who had cut off his own balls and tucked up his penis. Gai was small and thin, so he became a jockey."

Tom lit a cigarette from the butt of the last one before putting it out in the overflowing ashtray. I wrinkled my nose at the repulsive accumulation of butts and ashes. Laughing, he went on. "That's when he started shooting up. They all do it to stay small. He got hooked like everyone else, fucked up, and did some time. I got him out. He owes me."

He owes me. That's how everything works in Thailand. You give the guard in the parking garage twenty bahts, about fifty cents, and he owes you. You order a drink for a girl in a club, and she owes you. That's how it is.

"What do you know about the young Israeli woman who went missing?" I asked.

Tom looked at me, puffed on his cigarette to gain time, and said, "Look, we're friends. I'm nearing the end of the road on the force. I just came to say goodbye."

We sat in silence. I understood. You give twenty–thirty of the best years of your life to the system, and then one day something goes wrong. It isn't you who changed, it's the world around you. No one thinks or acts like you anymore. Suddenly you're a dinosaur with different standards, and then in a flash you're out on some lame excuse. I guess it's the same everywhere, not just where I come from. Guess? No, I know it is.

"What are you going to do?" I asked.

"Follow an old dream," he said with a grin. "I have some land in the south, not far from Phuket. I'm going to grow bananas, papaya, pineapple. I'll have a huge stable of gamecocks, for a little fun and some betting on the side. A quiet life. There'll be a cabin for you, too, somewhere you can bring a giggly little girl with a firm butt and do what every stupid *falang*, every white man, does in Thailand: eat, sleep, and make fucky-fucky all day. Not necessarily in that order."

I didn't want to tell him what I thought about his idiotic dream of going back to nature. First of all, in Thailand, unless you're Tom, you don't say what you think. If you do, you're considered a busybody. And if on top of that you show your emotions, people look at you funny. Secondly, there was no point. It was obvious it wouldn't last more than a year. That's all it would take for him to waste half of his retirement money on a worthless piece of land and the other half on ladyboys, his own kinky preference.

Besides, what could I do about it? Could I change how things played out or alter someone else's karma? I was only here to try to solve the mystery of one twenty-six-year-old Israeli woman who had gone missing.

If I were smarter, I would have known it didn't work like that in Thailand. Not for a *falang* like me. The conversation with Tom should have told me that sometimes the best answer is early retirement and a mediocre karma, even if it means that dreams are shattered and hopes are crushed. There are a lot of foreigners on the muddy bottom of the Chao Phraya River who thought they had gained an understanding of Eastern wisdom. But they were wrong. Very wrong.

"So you haven't heard anything about the disappearance of Sigal Bardon?" I tried again.

"No, and I don't want to. Capito?" Tom answered. "How many times can I hear about an Israeli who disappeared or got into trouble? As if you're the only ones here."

I wanted to believe him, but I wasn't convinced. Anyone who knows anything about the Bangkok police knows that the district commander has to keep himself informed of everything that happens in the city. If he takes his eye off the ball for a second, it can cost him dearly. Either in money or in power. And power is as valuable as money, sometimes more. The city doesn't sleep for a minute, and anyone who doesn't get on board on time misses the boat.

"Who am I working with here? Who should I talk to?

"Don't know, bro," he said. He used the Hebrew word *achi*, pronouncing it the way the Israeli kids on Khao San Road do, with the accent on the first syllable. "I wish I could give you a name, but you're on your own."

The car stopped in front of the Fontaine Hotel. Tom hadn't even asked. He knew I was staying there. It's where I always stay. True, there are nicer hotels in the city. The Hilton and the Shangri-La and the Hyatt. I have nothing against them. Why should I? I've spent quite a few pleasant hours sitting at the long bar in the Hyatt, for instance. But there's no other hotel in the whole city—let me say that again, no other—where you can open your window—if it opens at all and most of them don't—and breathe in the odors of the flesh market of Patpong. You can actually smell the sex games played by the young girls selling their wares.

What goes on outside your window isn't for the sensitive stomach of an innocent tourist who has come to see the sites and do some shopping. Anything can happen out there. You're all alone with only your instincts to rely on. Nighttime in Bangkok is not for the naïve.

Best advice: go to bed at a reasonable hour and turn the air conditioner on high to keep out the heat, the humidity, and the reek of sweat. And don't forget to lock the door and secure the safety chain.

* * *

Just across the street from the Fontaine Hotel is one of the oldest establishments devoted to *falang* entrapment. It's called Purple Octopus. For years it's been run by a skilled hustler named Yair Shemesh, a former Israeli known universally as Barbu, French for "bearded." I was probably the only one who still called him Yair. I found it hard to digest his current incarnation. I knew that sooner or later I'd have to cross the street, go up to the second floor, and see where things stood between us. We hadn't settled accounts for a long time, not since we had still been calling each other "cuz." I was hoping for later rather than sooner.

Tom and I got out of the car in the hotel parking lot, embracing like two weeping pussies. I remembered the Jameson and the cigarettes I was carrying, but Tom only took the cigarettes. "I have a feeling you're going to need the bottle more than me," he said. Taking out a pen, he wrote down a number. "This is Gai's cellphone," he said, pointing to the gaunt driver. "If you get into trouble, you know, the familiar kind when suddenly nobody knows you and everyone turns their back on you, give him a call and tell him where you are. He'll be there. You won't have to worry about anything else."

The white Toyota started to pull out and then stopped and reversed. Tom stuck his big ugly head out the window. "There're a lot of SOBs around," he warned. "They're young and ambitious, which makes them even worse bastards. Don't trust anyone. Not even the people on your side. Especially not the people on your side. Be careful."

I stood there like a schmuck. That's the only word for it. I waited until the roar of the engine faded and the Toyota disappeared among the hundreds of vehicles streaming down Silom Street. It wasn't that I was all alone. I'm used to that. Actually, I'm very good at it. It was that the people I knew, the people I counted on, the people who understood where I was coming from, were slowly vanishing into the chaos of collective forgetting—Was I also a part of that? For a moment, I just stood there. What for? Did I want Tom to come back, to talk to me, to rescue me? I was enveloped in a black cloud, a sort of personal prophecy that said the story of Sigal Bardon wasn't going to be just another case of an Israeli who went missing in a foreign city. I pulled myself together and went into the hotel, to the shadows awaiting me.

CHAPTER FOUR

I WOKE FROM a short nap. I had no reason to hurry, but since I was already awake, I dragged myself out of bed and into the shower. I'd developed the habit of taking a shower every chance I got in Thailand, where the degree of your whiteness—your *falangness*—was measured by the harshness of the smell from your armpits or the number of salt stains on your shirt. Besides, I thought, a tour of Patpong was always gratifying. Maybe not good for the health, but a feast for the eyes. What can I say? Human beings are a mass of contradictions.

It was early afternoon. I decided to walk. I needed to stretch my legs after the irritating flight and lack of sleep. Walking helps me think, too. Some people think best at a desk or over coffee and a cigarette. I need to be on my feet. The more I walk, the more my brain empties out and then the answers come and things fall into place. Even the questions become clearer. For the moment, I only had questions with no answers, and a single fact—Sigal Bardon was missing.

Questions:

Was Sigal alive?

If not, was she the victim of a random murder or was she targeted? Was she floating among the vegetation at the edge of one of the many canals that crossed Bangkok, or did someone take the trouble to hide the body?

If someone hid the body, then *who*? And *why*?

If she's alive, where is she? Is she hiding? If so, *where*? And *why*?

And most especially, *from whom*? That was the main question.

A lot of questions. But something else was bothering me. It took me a while to put my finger on it. I stopped short. A young woman coming out of a shopping center loaded down with bags almost ran into me. I kicked myself for being an idiot. It was staring me in the face, and I didn't see it. How did her family know that she was missing? Somehow, in the rush to get on a plane, I hadn't asked Shai, and he hadn't told me. An oversight on his part? I wasn't sure. For the time being, all I had was a gut feeling. But for someone who lives on clues and intuition, what else is there?

I texted Shai: *Who contacted us?*

My phone vibrated with his reply. *The family.*

Back to him: *How did they find out?*

He texted back: *Unknown source.*

That wasn't enough, I thought, filing the answer away for further consideration.

Expenses? I texted.

His response: *A hundred a day. No limit. But you need approval first.*

At least that gave me a certain degree of freedom. My legs kept carrying me up Silom Street, my mind calculating my next move.

* * *

Darkness came quickly, as it always does in the East. The bus stops were crowded with people at the height of the rush hour. Motorbike taxis darted madly among the slow-moving cars. Smoking three-wheeled tuk-tuks struggled to navigate among the other vehicles on the road until they, too, were stuck in the ever-growing gridlock that poured even more soot into the heavy haze that hung over the city. The Skytrain sped along its single elevated track, leaving a neon wake on the line of cars below.

I passed Lumpini Park, the green lung in the center of Bangkok, and began making my way back to the hotel, hoping my brain cells, deadened by the flight, would kick in. A cab pulled up beside me.

If it hadn't stopped, I probably would have kept walking. What changed my mind was the cold air that issued from the window when the driver rolled it down and called out "Taxi?"

I got in the back with a sigh of relief. Bangkok is a city of breaking points that you inevitably pay for dearly. The minute you buy something stupid you're never going to use; the fraction of a second when you smile at a girl in a bar, breaking rule number one: in the flesh market of the capital of sex games, always remain indifferent; the moment you get into a cab. Then it starts: "You want see pussy show? Pussy smoke cigarette? Pussy shoot ping-pong ball?"

The best answer a sensible tourist can give to such offers is *mai-ow*, don't want. That's the first thing you should learn from a Thai phrase book, and not the polite nonsense like *khob khun*, thank you, or *mai kao-jai*, I don't understand. *Mai-ow*. That's it.

But what tourist remains sensible in Bangkok? And who ever opens a phrase book these days?

I wasn't a tourist. As I said, I'd been coming here for twenty years, and thought I'd seen everything there was to see in Bangkok: the heavenly city above and its dark underbelly below, the human sewer. But you never know. The cold air from the AC began to get my lethargic mental juices flowing again. The driver was the usual shrimp. Small and jittery, with a long hair growing out of a mole on his chin, he was no different from most of the cabbies in Bangkok.

"Fontaine Hotel, Patpong," I instructed.

"Yes, yes," he said, glancing at me in the mirror with an expression that said "another *falang* moron who thinks he discovered Patpong."

We drove down Silom Street, passing the regular sights: young guys racing from store to store with earbuds stuck in their ears and bags with designer names in their hands; an occasional Western tourist standing on a corner with a map in his hand, not knowing that maps are worthless in Bangkok. You can't get anywhere on foot, and the moment you get into a cab, the driver will take you wherever he wants. It doesn't matter where you tell him to go; he has his own plans for you.

"First time in Bangkok?" the cabbie asked.

Really? I thought. "No, I've been here a few times before." *Go ahead, tell him I'd been coming and going for twenty years.*

"Business?"

Business. There is no word Bangkok cabbies like better. It has a universal meaning that immediately tells the driver how he can benefit from the innocent tourist in the back of his cab.

"Not this time," I said.

He sat in silence for a moment, before saying, "Bangkok like orchid. You like orchid?"

A poetic cab driver. He was starting to annoy me. That was a bad sign. If I'd been thinking straight, I might have realized how bad. But it's hard to think straight after a walk in Bangkok when you're dripping with sweat and your brain is at its boiling point—playing tricks on you.

"Not particularly," I said.

We were getting close to Patpong. From a main road like Silom Street, where we were now making our way from one traffic jam to the next, Patpong looks like all the other crowded markets filled with what my friend Tom liked to call *schmattes*. But when you get closer, you can see the girls standing outside the bars. Someone once called them the "caregivers of Patpong," but he didn't mean it in the medical sense.

"Many flowers in Bangkok," the driver said with a chuckle, catching my eye in the mirror. "Our flowers have scent."

"Their scent is the sweet smell of rot and corruption," I said.

"I see you know Bangkok well, sir."

"All I know," I answered, " is *tha di rab di; mi di rab mi di*— do good, get good; do bad, get bad."

He looked at me curiously. "You looking for boom-boom?"

I kept silent. I hadn't heard that expression in a long time. I guess we were from the same generation. Today they use different, more graphic, terms.

He seemed to be reading my mind.

"You not like our girls, no problem. You want fucky-fucky with white girl, I can arrange. Also, no problem. Look," he said, reaching into the glove compartment. "I have two passports. One very pretty girl. No want passports, want only my money. You take passports, you give me six hundred bahts. She give you what you want. I know."

When he bent over, I got a whiff of tiger balm, the hideous ointment that's a mixture of camphor and crushed tiger bones. It issued from his body, creating a lethal combination with the reek of Mekhong whiskey from his mouth. I was about to say something nasty when he held out two blue passports. Israeli passports.

I've seen plenty of passports in my day. And quite a few forgeries have passed through my hands. These two were legit. The picture hadn't been switched over a steaming electric kettle. They hadn't been faked by any expert either, and those were a dime a dozen in Bangkok. Along Khao San Road, where the backpackers congregate, every fourth or fifth store has a sign offering original student cards. In the storeroom in the back, there are passports for sale as well. Including Israeli ones. Dirt cheap.

The first passport bore the name Micha Waxman. And who looked out at me from the second one? *Sigal Bardon herself.* The young woman I'd been sent to find. The woman who went missing. The picture wasn't very flattering, and much less distinct than the one in the file Shai gave me, but there was no mistaking her. There wasn't a doubt in my mind.

I let out a soft whistle.

The clown thought it was a reaction to the exceptional beauty of the passport's owner. "Pretty girl," he said. "I take you?"

That's when I made the second mistake of the day. Breaking rule number two, I said, "Yes."

CHAPTER FIVE

I HANDED OVER the six hundred bahts, a bargain basement price for two genuine Israeli passports. Sixty shekels—just over seventeen dollars—about the cost of a blow job at the right bar, including a pint on the house. It was the least I'd ever paid for a passport. Even the fakes in Bangkok cost more.

I just happened to stumble on Sigal's passport? How implausible was that! The siren was going off in my head. I knew it wasn't blind luck. Everything in Bangkok happens for a reason. Someone had made sure it would end up in my hands.

I texted Shai from the cab: *Check out Micha Waxman. Ashdod. October '83.*

A couple of minutes later my phone vibrated. *17 hits. No criminal record.*

Micha Waxman, I thought, turning the name over in my head. Who was Micha Waxman? I knew nothing about him save for one thing: a Bangkok taxi driver had his passport, together with Sigal Bardon's.

"They get in my cab on Khao San," the driver said in reply to my question. "They want go to Hua Lamphong train station. They not have money. First, I think they lie. I very angry. Then I see they tell truth. The man, skinny. He shake all the time. I know drugs. He sweating. I even more angry. He make my cab wet. I very angry. They give me passports. No money. Keep passports, they say. I not want. The man sweating, disgusting. He say I come to Khao San another week, they come back, he give me money. Much money. I only want money for ride. Six hundred bahts. No want passports. No good. Police find, they not like."

That was some story. There are a lot of stories like that bouncing around Bangkok. I was a little skeptical about this one. For the moment, however, I decided to follow where it led, true or not. The fact is that when Israelis go overseas, they do the most unexpected things. It's sometimes hard to grasp the logic of their actions. It's as if stepping outside the borders of their home country releases some tightly wound spring. Everything gets shaken up and falls apart.

What were Sigal and Micha doing at the train station? Did they get on a train? Going where? On the face of it, it could be the usual story of Israeli backpackers taking the cheapest option: the night train to Surat Thani on the southern line to Hat Yai to save the cost of another night in a hotel, and from there a boat to Ko Pha-ngan, their favorite place to chill out and get high.

"Did they say where they were going?"

"Not know," the driver answered. "They speak language like mynah bird squawking." He made an attempt to imitate the guttural sound of the Hebrew letter *het*.

"What were they carrying?" I cut in. "Suitcase? Backpack?"

He thought for a minute. "Long bag. Big. Heavy. Sweating man not like carry. Want girl to help. She look angry. He shut mouth. Carry. Sweat." The driver laughed. "You *falang*, woman give look, man like chicken."

I gave him a murderous look that shut him up, and made a mental note to check out Hua Lamphong. I was familiar with the large train station on the city's main artery, Rama IV Road. Backpackers pass through it on their way south to the islands. Hopefully, Sigal and Micha had done something out of the ordinary enough for someone to remember them. The locals are used to the strange world of the backpackers—their scruffy appearance, lack of hygiene, rowdiness—but they'd notice something unusual. They were especially good at picking up on fear, maybe because in their own culture feelings are suppressed and hidden, never expressed out loud. The complete opposite of the Western world.

But from the file Shai prepared, Sigal Bardon didn't seem to be your typical backpacker. The family told him she had a tidy sum of money with her, along with credit cards from here to eternity. I got the picture of a spoiled brat, not the type who was likely to subject herself to discomfort to save money. But, of course, parents see their kids in a certain way, and they're inevitably surprised.

Backpackers all begin in the same place, at the same point of departure—the sporting goods stores that supply equipment and information. After that they go their separate ways. India, China, South America. Some have had enough after a month or two; others spend a year in India finding themselves and only come home when they run out of money. Some volunteer at the orphanages in Kolkata, and others get caught at the Bangkok airport on their way to Europe with a suitcase full of drugs.

I could put up flyers with Sigal's picture on Khao San Road, I thought, but I wasn't in love with the idea. For the time being, I preferred to work quietly, not send the message that someone was looking for her. Every message makes waves, and you never know where or who they'll reach.

What was in the heavy duffel bag? A duffel bag on a jaunt to the islands? It didn't smell right. I hoped it wasn't what I was starting to imagine. If Sigal got mixed up in drug running, it meant trouble.

*   *   *

The cab turned off the main road into one of the small side streets of the Banglamphu district. In the distance I could see the large blue Star of David on the Israeli Connection guest-house, a landmark for Israeli youngsters in Bangkok. I was sure that's where the driver was taking me—it was the obvious place—but he stopped a block before at a guesthouse called Shaya's Place. The name was so original it almost took my breath away, particularly since it was almost identical to the guesthouse on its right. And the one on its left. The restaurant, which opened onto the street, had blue plastic chairs and a sign in Hebrew that read: "Real Israeli shakshuka" and "Chopped green salad like your mama makes."

Out front, just like out front of every other guesthouse on the street, was a gathering of Israeli kids sporting earrings, dreadlocks, and tattoos on their arms and legs, in true tribal tradition. The ones who had already been to India and met a guru had enlightened names: Bodhi, Shanti Ram, Shanti Sita. Those just starting out on their adventure made do with humbler names: Bro or Sis.

Even before I got out of the cab, the flurry of activity I saw through the window strained my eyes. I climbed out, went inside, and crossed through the restaurant, brushing up against the local girls rushing from table to table to fill the demands of the fresh batch of noisy *falangs*. They may have just arrived, but they already knew where to sit, what to order—a Coke and steamed rice with vegetables—and, most importantly, how much to pay for it.

One of the girls looked up at me with a smile. In different circumstances, I would have paused for a moment, returned the smile, and said with the refined courtesy typical of the Thai people, "Sa *wat dee ka?*—how do you do?" Courtesy is the first, and maybe the major, key to the Thai culture. But I skipped it this time.

In the back was a flight of stairs. The lobby was dimly lit, with long shadows falling from the ceiling. A large notice board hung on one wall. An Israeli girl was standing in front of it, as absorbed as if she were reading the Bible.

"Looking for a partner for a trip to the islands. Leave a message. Noa"; "Anyone up for a trek to the northern tribes is welcome to join us. Leaving May 1"; "For sale: hiking boots and sleeping bag. Going home. Yonni. Green House"; "Anyone know where Sigal Bardon is? Weiss."

Anyone know where Sigal Bardon is? Weiss.

What was that all about? And who was Weiss? Someone was already looking for her. The note seemed innocent enough, but whoever pinned it here knew exactly what he was doing. I wrote down the telephone number. I wondered if it was real.

Then I texted the office: *Weiss? Israeli. Bangkok.*

I was just starting up the stairs when the reply came. It arrived in several fragmented messages.

Alex Weiss. In Thailand around five years.

Travels between Bangkok, Hong Kong, and Tokyo. Chain of stores selling knock-off watches.

Thai police and Interpol suspect they're a cover for Israeli drug ring in Southeast Asia.

Launders money in local real estate ventures, mainly around Pattaya.

The whistle I emitted this time was much quieter than the one I had let out in the cab. *Sigal*, I screamed silently, *what have you gotten yourself into? What have you brought on yourself? How does a woman who goes on a pleasure trip for a few months get mixed up with a guy like Alex Weiss?*

I went up to the second floor. The stairs led to a long corridor, as quiet and empty as a pharaoh's tomb. At the far end was a long batik curtain with pictures of the third eye of the Hindu god Shiva and other spiritual graffiti in vivid shades of purple, burgundy, yellow, and green. There was a light on behind it. I could make out someone moving in the shadows.

I pulled back the curtain to reveal a small room. Against the wall was a wooden desk lit by a single bulb. The man behind it was sitting on an executive chair that had seen better days—before the stuffing had started to burst through the upholstery. He was talking on the phone. There were two chairs on the other side of the desk. The rest of the office, if that's an appropriate word for what looked more like a storeroom, was piled high with cartons tied with thin rope. Here and there a piece of colorful fabric peeked out.

"Shaya?" I ventured.

Bingo.

He raised his eyes from the phone and looked at me for a second or two with cloudy red eyes. He didn't seem surprised.

"Hey there," he said, folding up a scrap of newspaper with weed sticking out of the ends and shoving it into a drawer. He was thirtysomething, but did his best, without much success, to look younger: a scruffy beard cut once a week with a hair trimmer, thin sideburns, and an unbuttoned shirt revealing a large Star of David hanging low on his chest from a heavy gold chain and indicating exactly where he came from.

"What?" he asked wearily. It was obvious he wasn't in the mood for talking.

"I'm looking for someone," I said.

"And?"

I ignored the lack of empathy, attributing it to the joint whose odor still hung in the air. I wished I could open a window, but there weren't any.

"Her name is Sigal Bardon."

His murky eyes came alive, but only for a very brief moment. It was as if he hastened to turn his interest off with an internal switch.

"I'll check my records," he said.

It took him a minute or so to make some semblance of order out of the papers on the desk. Finally, he pulled out a jumbled pile of coffee-stained forms divided into numbered squares representing the rooms in his establishment. Leafing through them, he chose one dog-eared sheet, presumably the most recent.

He looked it over and then raised his eyes. "We don't usually give out information about our guests." I leaned against the wall. Of course, I could have reached over and grabbed him by the ear, but it was still early in the day. The image of the sweet smile of my seatmate on the plane, on her way to a Vipassana course in Bangkok, was still fresh in my mind. The memory of her innocence made me feel charitable. I didn't want to get my hands dirty yet.

In retrospect, that was my third mistake of the day. If I'd crushed the bug's face on the wall right then and there, fewer bodies may have been found floating in the muddy waters of the Chao Phraya River.

"You know the law in Thailand as well as I do," I said. "The military junta gives drug dealers the death penalty without the benefit of trial." I could see the hatred, and fear, in his eyes. Fear is an excellent fuel for hatred. Anyone who has spent any time in Bangkok, particularly on its fringes, knows that Thai cops don't play around. Clearly, Shaya and I were never going to be friends. "Room 208," he hissed through clenched teeth. "The other building, in the back."

"Thanks," I said. "You're a pal, Shaya. You can be real nice when you want to." I'd made my first enemy on this trip. On average, not bad for the start of an investigation. I knew that the moment I left he'd take the little package out of the drawer and prepare the fastest-rolled joint ever in the history of the East. He might also do some speed for good measure. What I didn't know was that after his first drag on the joint, he'd press a button on his phone and in a smoke-choked voice, he'd say, "Someone was just here looking for her."

CHAPTER SIX

NARROW IRON STEPS led down into the alley. I passed an open kitchen where a cook was chopping vegetables with a large knife while chatting with the dishwasher, who scrubbed dishes in a big plastic basin with the help of a lot of water, a little soap, and a rag that had been demoted after years of service wiping tables.

The alley was the epitome of a back street in Bangkok: tiny boxlike plywood houses; open doors to let in some light and air; laundry hanging from wires stretched along the walls and held in place by two nails. Famished flea-ridden dogs lay semi-conscious in the shade provided by a wagon with flat tires. Two children played with a bicycle rim. In the middle of the alley, between the wooden houses, was an open Muay Thai boxing ring, a large arena with a small raised platform marked off by ropes, and pictures of local heroes, champions who had started out in this very place. Boxing gloves and shorts hung from a rack. It was like thousands of other arenas throughout Thailand. Two young men were honing their skills on punching bags, while several others sat on low stools in the shade of a huge ficus tree, eating from bowls of steamed rice, stir-fried vegetables, strips of meat coated in sesame seeds, and small cubes of meat in a sauce that gave off the strong odor of chili. Beside them was a big bottle of Mekhong whiskey, nearly empty.

They fell silent when I passed, looking at me with blank, sealed expressions. That was fine by me. I wasn't expecting a smile from every person on the street. It's only the two-dimensional people on the billboards that follow you from the second you land at the airport that are always smiling.

One of the men came toward me. He was a short broad-shouldered chap in yellow shorts over muscle-bound thighs that looked like they'd been molded from cement. "Want fight?" he asked with a grin, revealing black teeth. He made boxing gestures to demonstrate. "Maybe later," I said like a stupid tourist instead of just keeping quiet and moving on.

Sometimes the little traps are the most dangerous. You fall into them when you drop your guard for a second, and you always pay the price in the end.

*   *   *

The three-story building in the back had suffered the ravages of time, its walls stained by dark patches of mold from the monsoon rains. Narrow wooden stairs led from one floor to the next. On the first floor were rooms, if that's a suitable name for the cramped tiny spaces separated by plywood that kept nothing out, not roaches, not spiders, and not the sound of people fucking at night. A room cost two hundred bahts, all a typical Israeli backpacker could afford on their limited budget. A girl emerged from one of the rooms and headed toward the communal shower carrying a towel and soap.

I was about to try the friendly approach when I saw the look of loathing on her face. I suspected it was a reflection of the humiliation she was suffering now that all the great guys she had joined up with in India only had eyes for Thai girls with their cute butts and little pussies, leaving her to go shave her pits in frustration and blame her tour of duty in the Israel Defense Forces for her big ass.

Room 208 was at the end of the hall. I knocked on the thin plywood board purporting to be a door. No answer. I stuck my ear against it and knocked again. Nothing. But I could tell there was someone inside. I knocked harder.

"Who's there?" came an apprehensive voice behind the door.

"I'd like to talk to you."

"What do you want?" There was fear in the voice now. "I don't have it. Tell him I don't have it."

"Stop whining. I've got your passport," I said.

The door was opened just as far as the rusty metal chain would allow.

I've seen junkies in bad shape, but he was in a worse state than most. Micha Waxman was definitely not the sweet dream of every Jewish mother. He was her deepest, darkest nightmare. The sort of thing you can only expect from the neighbor's loser son. The kid peering out at me had a skeletal unshaven face that was sweaty and jaundiced. He looked at the passport in my hand.

"I'm sick, man," he said. "I don't have any money. Come back tomorrow. My parents are wiring me money."

"I don't want your money, Micha," I said. "I want to talk to you."

"Leave me alone. Can't you see I'm hurting?" He tried to close the door, but my foot was already blocking it, and the metal chain wouldn't do much good either.

He moved back.

"I'll give you the passport. Promise."

He held out a skinny hand. His whole arm was dotted with needle marks and broken veins.

"Hold on," I said. "First I want to know where Sigal Bardon is."

"I don't know who you're talking about." He was obviously scared. If there's one good thing about heroin withdrawal it's that it makes it impossible to lie. Not well, anyway.

"C'mon, Micha," I said. I was still keeping my tone amiable, but I was beginning to feel my good mood slipping away.

"I swear," he said, "on my mother's life." He clutched at the thin gold hamsa hanging from a chain around his neck and kissed it. I could see he was going to start crying if I pushed any harder, but I had no choice. I gave the door a shove. The rusty chain broke off. I grabbed his arm and twisted it slightly. He was such a wimp I knew just a little physical pain could be effective, but I wasn't expecting the show he put on. He started screaming "ow" and "Mommy"—it's interesting how your mother always shows up at times like this—and wept tears the size of monsoon raindrops. It was repulsive, too much for me to take. I'd already let go of his arm. What with all the bodily fluids leaking from it, I was worried I'd catch something ugly.

"Quit it," I said. "Calm down or I'll slap you."

I found a small face towel on the bed and picked it up gingerly—God only knew what microbes were growing on it—and handed it to him.

I'm not a violent guy by nature. On the contrary. I don't think I got in more than one or two fights when I was a kid.

But in the counterterrorism unit in the Army, I learned to use my arms and legs as supplementary weapons, or at least to hurry things along. Later, when I worked for the Security Agency, I polished my skills. Physical abuse became an interrogation tool. I found it useful, but I didn't get any pleasure out of violence, neither mine nor anyone else's. Well, maybe just a little.

I was dripping in sweat. It was flowing in rivers down my arms and neck. The room was hot, and the small revolving fan on the brown wood chest of drawers in the corner was stuck in one position, not doing any good whatsoever.

Micha wiped his face, pulled himself together, and sat down on the bed that was pushed up against the wall.

"Where is Sigal, Micha?" I asked again.

"I don't know anything," he answered. "I don't know where she is. She hit me up for some dope. We shared it. That's all. I swear. That's all. She was only here for a second. Then she disappeared. Look, her stuff is still here," he said, pointing to a small brightly colored pouch, the kind the kids pick up in Nepal.

"Li-ar," I said, drawing out the syllables to make it sound threatening.

He started shaking again, a sign either of fear or withdrawal. It didn't matter. The more he shook, the more aggravated I got.

"You went to the train station with her," I said, coming closer. "What did you do there?"

He covered his face with his hand to fend off a slap. "I have nothing to do with it. Leave me alone. She asked me to help her with the bag."

The small cloth pouch Sigal had left behind was open. I rummaged through it: light cotton clothes, a few fashionable lacy bras, mostly black, high-end brands—I understand that sort of thing—thongs, an open box of tampons, a toiletry kit, a cosmetic bag.

"What was in the other bag?"

I'd lost him. Micha Waxman was sitting on the bed staring at me wide-eyed. He was sweating profusely, wiping his face over and over with the filthy little towel.

"You're not gonna hurt me?"

I didn't answer him immediately. I did a tour of the room to make sure I hadn't missed anything.

"Are you a dealer," I asked, "or just a dumbass user?"

He pulled back even further until he was up against the wall.

"You're on your way to the Bangkok Hilton," I told him. "And once you're there, you don't leave so soon, if ever."

I turned to leave. Suddenly, he came alert. "Aren't you gonna give me my passport?"

"We'll see," I said as I walked out.

I needed fresh air. There was no question the little shithead knew more than he was saying, but heroin had sent him off into other lands. I'd have to catch him off guard when he wasn't strung out, I thought, exiting the building.

* * *

I started making my way back up the alley. Just before I reached the boxing arena, my path was blocked. The broad-shouldered boxer with the short legs and yellow shorts grinned, again revealing his rotten teeth. If he'd been alone, I might have given him a reason to see the dentist, but he wasn't, so I didn't put up any opposition. It was better to get it over with quickly. They all had cement legs, without any feeling or nerves, and it wouldn't make any difference to them if I managed to land a punch or two.

Muttering *falang kai nuk*—white men are bird shit—one of them punched me in the stomach. It was the type of blow that doesn't leave a bruise. The air was knocked out of me, and I couldn't breathe. Another guy kicked me while I was down and said in a mixture of Thai and English, "*Falang*, go home." His meaning was utterly clear despite the heavy accent.

The bastards didn't even bother to leave. That was their righteous spot, under the sacred ficus tree. They sat back down and poured themselves another round of Mekhong, not so much as glancing in my direction. Someone had told them to give me the old one-two, just a taste, to see how tough I was. So that's what they did.

Someone was sending me veiled messages, and I don't like that. Even in our dark world you ought to make yourself clear. Who was behind it?

But I didn't take it to heart, even though my ribs hurt. I hoped they weren't cracked. You can't take anything to heart in Bangkok. If you don't keep your cool, you won't last long in a country where for a few bahts you can hire a pack of bullies to beat up a foreigner. They probably didn't even know why. All they cared about was earning enough for another cheap bottle of Mekhong.

* * *

When I got back to the street, the annoying cab driver was still there, waiting for me.

"You see her?" he asked.

"Fuck off," I said. I wondered who he was working for.

He didn't let it go. "You *falangs* come here, think you very smart. Think you know Thailand. You not know nothing. *Falang* like bird shit. White and thick."

I wasn't eager to use the services of the poetic driver again. I didn't have the slightest doubt he hadn't fallen out of the sky but had been sent by someone, even if I still didn't know who. But my whole body ached.

"You're not the first person to tell me that today," I said collapsing onto the back seat, my hands pressing against my painful ribs.

CHAPTER SEVEN

FISHING FOR CLUES means you're sometimes forced to play nice with the powers that be. I can't say that's my forte, but it's part of the job. The following afternoon I set out for the Israeli embassy, deliberately timing my visit so I'd be there toward the end of office hours.

Even from a distance I could see the armed cops keeping an eye on all the adjacent corners and crossings. The building itself was surrounded by a high wall fitted with cameras and floodlights. You have to push a button on the gate to speak to the guard in the next layer of security. I leaned on the button, which always irritates them.

"Good morning," a voice answered. "How can I help you?"

"I'm Dotan Naor. I'd like to talk to the head of security."

"Please stick your passport in the crack," the metallic voice instructed.

"You sure you don't want me to stick something else in it?" I said.

It was a long time before I got a response, but eventually I heard a voice I recognized immediately. "Same old Dotan, I see. Same old lame jokes."

The voice belonged to Shmulik. What the hell was he doing here? Head of embassy security? There was no doubt in my mind he was standing in front of the security camera laughing at me, very pleased with himself.

"Don't let that loser in," his voice echoed through the speaker. But the chuckle that accompanied it was hesitant enough for me to identify the question in his head: How much does he—that is, me—know?

I heard the buzzer, pushed open the gate, and entered the guard post. He was checking my passport. "Any weapons?" he asked.

"No."

"Second floor. You'll find it. The entrance is at the end of the garden."

It didn't take long for me to realize that Shmulik had become a common variety security chief. There may not be a guidebook like the ones you use to identify local flora or fauna, but security chiefs are just as easy to categorize. Those who used to work for the Security Agency are a little over the hill. The Foreign Ministry is happy to hire them at the first sign of a pot belly, but don't let the extra weight in front deceive you. They may no longer solve problems with an elbow to the kidneys or a kick in the gut, but they haven't gotten soft or complacent. Just smarter. They still keep things close to the chest and don't hesitate to lie when necessary.

Shmulik's office was identical to that of every other security chief in the world, and I've seen a lot of them. A stark room with a telephone, thin-screen computer, and a few small Israeli flags. On the wall behind him were pictures of the President and Prime Minister, which were periodically switched out. Photos of his ex-wife and two girls, freckled smiling redheads, sat on his desk. The ex, by the way, wasn't smiling. I wondered why. But I was more interested in the board with the details of missing persons on the wall.

I knew I was raw meat for him. He could chop me up any way he wanted. This was his moment, and he was going to savor it. It wasn't what he'd been looking forward to in the lazy afternoon hours. He would have preferred a cup of tasteless coffee, even cold coffee that had been sitting on his desk for a long time, to a ghost from the past. But now that I was here, he was going to make the most of it.

Shmulik was a large man, a mountain you couldn't ignore, especially given the bald egg-shaped head above a thick bullish neck. The strength of this human mass was apparent even when he was sitting behind a standard desk with his blue uniform jacket hanging over the back of the chair, his obligatory tie loosened, and his shirtsleeves rolled up far enough to show what was left of the bulging muscles he once had. His eyes were gray-blue, like a fish. They were eyes that had learned not only to see, but to scrutinize and probe. He was sipping coffee, none too quietly, I might add.

He stood up and shook my hand across the desk. "The security camera at the gate didn't do you justice," he said. "It didn't show how good-looking you are."

Despite the AC, his hand was damp and clammy, maybe because of all the coarse black hair that covered the back of it. You could polish shoes with it. When he stood, I could see that he was starting to get thick around the waist, like many muscle-bound men do when they reach middle age.

He sat back down, or more accurately, dropped heavily back onto his chair, and pointed to the one on my side of the desk. "Have a seat," he said.

I sat. He examined me. There wasn't a drop of friendliness in his eyes. "Okay, Dotan, what're you doing here?"

"Taking a little break," I said.

My answer neither interested nor irked him. You can't evoke emotion from people like Shmulik. They couldn't care less. "So what happened to your face on your little break?"

His question made me realize that my jaw was sore. I passed my hand over it. My cheek was swollen. The midgets in the alley had done more damage than I thought. I hadn't even taken the time to look in the mirror.

"I drank too much last night. Fell on my face," I said.

"You still think everyone else fell off the cabbage truck?"

"I hear there're a lot of cabbages in Bangkok." It wasn't the wittiest comeback in the world, but that's all I could come up with on the spur of the moment. I can usually do better.

"So what're you doing here?" he repeated.

Getting up, he paced the room. I knew him well enough to know he was trying to figure out how to get me to sing. I waited. There was no hurry.

"It was raining, so I popped in for a visit." That was true, at least in part. The first part. It was drizzling outside, and I kept thinking of all the shit that would come floating up.

"Okay, fine," he said. "So we'll start at the beginning. I understand you've already been to Shaya's Place."

"Who have you got there?" I asked. "Shaya himself?"

Me and my big mouth. If I could only learn to keep it shut. Especially with guys like Shmulik, who was no less seasoned than me. If I hadn't asked the question, I might have milked the answer out of him. It could just as well be Weiss, for instance.

But whether deliberately or not, Shmuel diverted me from that line of enquiry. "If I don't know what's going on in my

Israeli community, then who does? Every day I get another planeload of weirdos of every size and shape you can imagine. Every one of them is here to find their own pot of gold at the end of the rainbow, and find it fast. And they're all convinced they'll be welcomed with open arms. One wants to invest in a whorehouse, another wants to open a club. One gets caught at the airport with a kilo of heroin and another with ten cobras and three little Burmese pythons in his bag. And that's without even counting the twenty-thousand-plus backpackers a year who arrive loaded down with ganja from Goa, Manali, or Dharamsala. You wouldn't believe what a jungle it is out there."

I nodded, although he was tiring me out with his list. But Shmulik wasn't done. It wasn't every day he got a visitor he could badger.

"Just yesterday they bring me a certified goody two-shoes. On the plane from Delhi he went into the toilet, stuffed a rag in the smoke detector, and smoked joint after joint rolled in toilet paper. In the end, there was so much smoke that it set off the alarm. I ask him, 'Tell me, what were you thinking? Don't you know it's against the law? You know what kind of fine you're gonna pay?' And what does he say? This kid with thirty earrings and dreadlocks down to his waist? He gives me a big smile and says, 'I had some weed left. I didn't want to throw it out, and I thought it would be cool to chill out during the flight.' Cool. And every time I have to come up with some explanation for the local cops, one guy in the Tourist Police in particular, Major Somnuk. You don't want to meet him. Every time I have to explain they're good kids right out of the Army who're just testing the limits of cool."

I didn't give a shit about his problems. We all have our own burdens to bear, and right now mine was a woman named

Sigal Bardon who seemed to have disappeared into thin air, and the clock was ticking. The only thing I knew for sure was that she was somewhere in Thailand without a passport and probably without any friends if she had to get help from a drughead like Micha Waxman.

I went over to the board of missing persons. There were a few photos on it. I checked them out one by one, reading the notations below. Eyal P., last seen in northern Laos. Three months later, someone tried to sell his passport and camera on Khao San. Idit S., went for a boat ride on Tonlé Sap Lake in Cambodia. By the looks of it, she fell in the water when her boat collided with another one. They searched for two weeks. Body not found. Micha A., went on a trek alone in northern Thailand. Might have accidentally crossed the border into Myanmar.

There were more photos. All the faces were young, attractive, smiling. The info was gathered from every hole in Southeast Asia where Israelis go and for which the security chief in Bangkok is responsible. What happens to all these kids? How is it that they attract disaster and death like magnets?

There was no sign of Sigal Bardon on the board.

"Impressive list," I said. "Is it up-to-date?"

A few seconds of silence passed between us. Shmulik glanced at the papers on his desk and then raised his eyes to me. "I'm guessing you're expecting me to offer you coffee," he said, and called to the woman in the adjacent office, "Aliza."

A woman poked her head in the door before coming in. Young, late twenties maybe early thirties. As cute as a button. Bright face, almost glowing. A mass of blond hair wound into a bun on top of her head. She was dressed in a green blouse that looked casual but was undoubtedly from one of the top designers, and, of course, she wasn't wearing a bra. In the light from the window on the opposite wall, her breasts were a sight to behold. Perfect pears. I wondered whether Shmulik had anything to say about them. Probably not, or maybe he was used to them because I didn't see his eyes wandering. Inside her tight jeans, I could imagine a pair of legs it wouldn't hurt to gaze at.

The look in her black eyes seemed to imply I'd said a dirty word.

"I didn't know you had a friend," she said, turning her attention to Shmulik.

"Don't worry, he doesn't," I said.

We all laughed. Shmulik, not so heartily.

"I bet you're an academic," Aliza said, "doing your PhD on Buddhist sculpture from the Khmer period. You're here doing field work and chalking up expenses for tax purposes."

"How did you know? Woman's intuition?"

We laughed again, just the two of us this time. Progress. I thought how nice it would be to sit with her in the evening on the long bar of the Hyatt Hotel and check out the state of the bottle of whiskey I'd left there last time. They play good music in the bar in the evening.

"Forgive me for breaking up this intimate moment," Shmulik said. "Aliza, would you mind making coffee? Two?"

Ignoring him, she said, "My shift is over at five. That's when the uniform comes off." With a laugh, she disappeared back into her office.

"You're still the same letch you always were," Shmulik said. "Isn't it time to settle down?"

"Nowadays they call it appreciating women. Besides, you know relationships are always painful for me."

From beneath his accustomed cynicism, I'd managed to elicit a genuine laugh. That was my chance.

"Tell me, Shmulik," I said, changing the subject, "what do you know about Sigal Bardon?"

"More trouble," he answered.

"We've always got trouble. It's our existential state. We're used to it. But I'm convinced this woman's story is different."

"What's your interest in her?"

I rubbed my swollen face gently. "If there's one thing I don't like it's when people mess with me."

"That's not an answer." Shmulik wasn't going to let up.

"Her family hired us," I said.

"You make money out of other people's problems?"

"In a way," I said, not defending myself. "Who doesn't?"

There was an icy look in his gray-blue eyes. I could see the muscles in his arms twitching from the pressure on the nerves running through them. I knew I only had a few minutes left before he got fed up with the game and tossed me out of his office.

He resumed his official manner. "Nothing new, not a single clue to go on. You know the local cops."

Know was one way to put it.

"Who's handling the case?" I asked.

"Major Somnuk from the Tourist Police. He's not the most good-tempered person around, to put it mildly." Chuckling, he added, "I imagine you'll run into him at some point."

Aliza came back with the coffee. The ass she flaunted was for my sake. This time we parted with a broad smile.

"What do you know about Alex Weiss?" I asked Shmulik.

His cold eyes flashed. He was about to say something when the telephone rang. He listened intently, throwing me a glance from time to time. Finally, he said into the phone, "I can't leave now. I'll decide what to do about it." He hung up and turned to me. "That's it, Dotan. Get outta here. Something just landed on me. You can't say I didn't try to be nice even though you've been fucking with me for an hour."

I finished the coffee. You learn to sip on your coffee slowly, knowing that the timing of the final sip is very important. You can never tell what's going to happen just before you put your cup down. Like now, when Aliza came in again. It didn't require any effort to read the name on the cover of the file she was holding: Sigal Bardon.

"Can I have a look?" I asked Shmulik.

"I'm putting it on my desk. I don't owe you a thing, but I have to take a leak. You're not here when I get back."

The file contained two sheets of paper and some old photos, mostly family pictures. I leafed through them. Scribbled on a small colored note, held on with a paper clip, were the words "Reut Bardon, Oriental Hotel, Room 339."

That was enough.

I left the office. On my way out, I saw Aliza at her desk, talking on the phone. She waved to me, but the smile on her face didn't match the cold look in her eyes.

CHAPTER EIGHT

A DAY IN Bangkok is like a week anywhere else. In a lot of ways. So I wasn't surprised when the cab was waiting for me outside the embassy.

It's nice to see that someone's looking out for you. But it's not so nice when you don't know who it is. Like a leech, the ubiquitous driver was starting to feel attached to me. He wanted to know if I'd already had some fucky-fucky today. For my part, I just wanted to get rid of him. But cabbies think they know better than you where you're going, and especially where you *want* to go. This one in particular. He seemed to know where to take me even before I opened my mouth.

I kept up the cat and mouse game he'd begun. Obviously, I was bothered by the fact that he stuck to me like glue, but I could take care of him later if it became necessary.

"You tell me when you get fucky-fucky," he said, interrupting my train of thought. He threw me a lascivious grin. "How many time your sea cucumber go in and out before it squirt?"

"I never counted."

My answer didn't satisfy him. "How many hour it go?" he asked. "Thai man like Superman. Drink one, two bottle like this," he said. He reached over to the glove compartment and took out one of the small square amber-colored bottles sold legally at every 7-Eleven. It was a steroid drink of one kind or another. "It call Lipo. Make it go all night. Three hundred bahts. You want?"

He was going to be my supplier, too? It made me wonder. How far would he go?

When I didn't respond, he pulled out another bottle. "This call Krating Daeng. Only two hundred. Work good, too. You want?"

I ignored him, but he didn't give up. He suggested I rest up for a couple of hours and then he'd come and take me to some places he knew.

"*Mai-ow*," I said. Don't want.

He gave me a puzzled look. I'd finally managed to shut the shrimp's mouth. Or at least I thought I had.

A small gilt Buddha was hanging from the rearview mirror. Wound around it was a thin chain from which a triangular amulet dangled. The driver undid it and held it out to me.

"Take," he said. "It from Buddha of the West."

I raised a quizzical eyebrow. Who or what was he referring to?

On the clay amulet was a crude relief of Buddha.

"It have much power," he explained. "It do anything, except stop bullet."

People in Thailand believe in countless superstitions. It's rare to see one without some kind of amulet around their neck. Amulets, what they call *phra krueng*, have the magical power to protect, cure, and strengthen. Some people wear one, while others have a mass of chains hanging from their neck, each with a different amulet. The most popular one, of course, is

Buddha. It doesn't matter if it's made of wood, stone, or clay, as long as some monk blessed it and it's said to have strong power.

"You should have," the driver said. "I see dangerous aura around you. No good. No healthy."

I took a stack of bills out of my pocket. "How much?"

He threw me a glance in the mirror. He didn't seem offended, just surprised at my lack of manners. "No mine. You only borrow."

Amulets have sacred value. That's why they're not bought and sold, only borrowed from a stall or seller. Without giving it much thought, I slipped it around my neck. It felt pleasantly cool. As soon as I put it on, I forgot about it, and maybe that was the whole point. It was there without my being aware of it. And like my mother used to say, even if it doesn't help, it can't hurt.

I told the driver to take me to the train station. Like cabbies all over the world, he started whining about how bad traffic was at this time of day and how it would be stop and go the whole way. I put another five hundred bahts on the seat beside him. This time he kept his mouth shut until we got there.

I got out at the station and tried to imagine what a man and woman dragging a heavy bag, which I assumed was filled with drugs, would do. The station was deserted. The night trains had already left. The popular train to Surat Thani in the south had left at five thirty-three. I wondered how many stupid *falangs* were sitting on it right now, shaking in fear that someone might inspect their bag.

I strode from the ticket booths through the large hall to the platform. The corridor was lined with lockers of all sizes. Was the bag on its way out of Bangkok, or was it hidden away in one of the lockers?

It's easy to find foreigners outside Bangkok. They stand out against the background. But for some reason I was almost certain that if Sigal was still alive, she was in the city. I envisioned her hiding out somewhere, scared to death. Unless it was too late for the scared part, leaving only death.

I stood in the middle of the station for a few minutes, knowing I had reached a dead end. That happens in investigations, no reason to get upset. You keep digging and something else pops up. Something happens. Clearly, I had started making waves, and they'd get bigger. Of course, they could also come back and hit me in the ass.

* * *

When I got back to the hotel, the lobby was buzzing with activity and filled with the usual noise of guys who'd brought local girls with them for a night of fun and were haggling with the manager over the cost of changing the room to "double occupancy." One of them followed me into the elevator with a dark girl on his arm. She stood facing the door with her eyes lowered, carrying a small purse that most likely held her identity card, a cheap lipstick, chewing gum, a little cash, and, with any luck, a condom or two.

"You couldn't find one?" the guy asked me with a wink. He was the type who slapped a whore on the ass in a Bangkok hotel elevator, the type who went abroad with two wads of bills wrapped in rubber bands. Five thousand to buy a present for his wife, a gold bracelet or necklace with semi-precious gems so she wouldn't ask questions about what he did in Bangkok, and another ten to burn. But he still haggled with the hotel manager over the twenty-five bucks he was being charged for "double occupancy," and he'd still say he was being robbed. "You don't have to look hard around here," he informed me. "They fall on you like flies. When I'm through with her you can take her for a ride if you want. I'll go get another one in Patpong later. Whaddaya say?"

"We'll see," I answered.

"No problem. Whenever you want. Don't be bashful. We Israelis have to look out for each other here, right?"

* * *

The bottle of Jameson worked particularly well that night. I took a shower and then poured myself a generous glass and sat down by the window. Across the way, the flashing neon sign screamed Purple Octopus. I thought about the Israelis in Bangkok. What were they looking for? My mind turned to Yair Shemesh—Barbu—and I wondered how he came to be the manager of such a place. What had happened between leaving the Security Agency and ending up here? The one time I saw him after we parted ways, I didn't ask him. I knew I should pay him a visit and question him about Sigal Bardon. A man like him knows things. But not tonight. At that moment, I wasn't even capable of picking myself up out of the chair. The mental effort of crossing the street, going into the club, and watching dull-eyed girls dance on metal poles was too much for me. Flashing neon signs might be tempting, but they didn't call to me that night.

CHAPTER NINE

I WAS AWOKEN early in the morning by the chanting of mantras coming from a group of monks passing below my window. *Namo tassa bagawato arahato samma sambuddhassa*—Honor to the Blessed One, the Exalted One, the fully Enlightened One. I imagined them walking barefoot with their beggar's bowls and contemplating how to rid themselves of the filth known as life on earth. Sighing, I turned over. After so many visits to the East, I was just beginning to understand that people like me had a lot of incarnations ahead of us before we learned not to get caught on the hook called suffering.

I looked at my watch. Four thirty in the morning. Those guys were nuts. I took a few sips from the bottle of water on the nightstand, turned the AC up to freezing, and went back to sleep. The next time I woke up, sunlight was already streaming through the large windows. Naturally, I'd forgotten to draw the curtains. I picked up the phone and asked the operator to connect me to the Oriental Hotel, Room 339. And that was even before I had my coffee.

The female voice that answered was clear and pleasant.

"My name is Dotan Naor," I said.

There was a moment of silence before she said, "I know who you are."

"I'd like to talk to you."

"Can you come here? I'm at the Oriental," she said.

"I know. I just called you."

More silence. Finally, "I'll be in the café."

"I'll be there in fifteen minutes," I said.

* * *

Since its establishment, the café at the Oriental has been the best place to sit, ponder life, and watch the Chao Phraya flow by. Nothing much has changed since Joseph Conrad assumed his first command of the Otago and sailed into the huge channel, or, as an old salt once referred to it, "the river, aye . . . a strange bit of water."

The wide river flowed gently toward the bend in the south. It bustled with activity: large barges loaded down with sand and gravel, nearly sinking below the waterline, were dragged along by small, industrious tugboats; elegant long-tail boats, their motors roaring, slithered among the floating islands of blue water hyacinths and cut dangerously in front of the barges; ungainly ferry boats crossed the river at the narrowest point, carrying passengers back and forth between the Thonburi district on one side and the center of Bangkok on the other; the crowded water buses lumbered from stop to stop, the orange robes of the monks on deck visible from afar, sending a message of peace and moderation to a restless, sometimes perilous world.

She was sitting at a table on the terrace overlooking the river.

"Dotan," I introduced myself.

She raised her eyes, shielding them from the sun with her hand despite the large white parasol that shaded the wooden table. Her big and bright eyes were a striking deep green. We shook. The handshake lasted a second too long. Both of us sensed it.

"Reut."

We laughed. Apparently, the formalities were over.

A waiter arrived at the table and checked me out from head to toe. My jeans and sneakers were not in keeping with the Oriental Hotel, not even by the pool. Reut ordered iced coffee. I was about to ask for a double espresso, but said instead, "I'll have a gin and tonic."

Not my drink at all. And certainly not in the morning. But there's nothing like a G&T beside the calming rhythmic flow of water. We sat and watched the river. It was almost pastoral.

"It's a lovely time of day," Reut said. "Maybe the nicest in Bangkok. Later it gets too hot."

Her voice painted a picture, as if a delicate brush moved through the air when she spoke, sketching the scene as she described it. For a moment, the world could only be seen in one way—through her eyes. The palm trees among the tables in the café waved gently in the morning breeze, their branches dancing in an enchanting undulating motion. The river shimmered like a mirror in metallic blue. There was no sense of urgency. I took another sip and marveled. It was the usual gin, the usual bubbly tonic, the usual lemon, although it was probably a lime. Everything else came from her.

She bore a certain resemblance to her sister, and yet she appeared to be the antithesis of the woman I imagined from

Sigal's pictures. She was wearing a summery dress, and on the chair beside her was a straw hat with a bandanna around the brim, the sort of hat European women wear when they go on safari. Dark sunglasses lay next to it. Except for her nails, painted the brightest red I had ever seen, Reut looked as far as possible from a pickup girl, and there wasn't the slightest hint of any "come-hither" look in her eyes. Her beauty was refined and restrained. Tiny drops of perspiration, like dewdrops, stood on her brow just below the hairline. I yearned to be a hummingbird flitting around her, oblivious to the rest of the world.

"From here it looks like we're in paradise," she said.

"Not from where I'm sitting," I answered.

She let that sink in, throwing me a glance but in no hurry to reply. To an onlooker we may have seemed like a couple who had already said all there is to say in a single life cycle and were now sitting and watching the river flow by, musing about its journey from where it rises to where it splits in the delta.

"Tell me about yourself," she said.

I didn't answer her immediately. I lit a cigarette. A Camel. I don't do that very often. I've never been a serious smoker, but I always have a pack in my pocket for those moments when I feel the need for the decadent taste of tobacco.

I took two long puffs, and then, with the smoke rising in the air beside the muddy river, I turned to her. "My resume is nothing special. Not a lot to tell. I had a government job in security and now you might say I'm taking some time off."

"A long time?"

"That's still up in the air."

"It didn't end well?" she asked, patting her face with a wet wipe she took from the purse on the chair beside her.

"One day I found myself high up on a shaky ladder," I said somewhat belligerently, irritated by the directness of her question. "It's not a position you can maintain for a long time. Either you straighten up or you fall."

She gave me a searching look before asking, "What do you know about my family?"

"From what I read, you're rich and you're divorced. You used to be married to a man named Nimrod Merhav, who also came from money. At some stage, he disappeared from the picture. Your father is a wealthy industrialist. Your sister . . ." I fell silent. The intrusive waiter was standing by our table, asking if I wanted another drink. I nodded.

"Go on," she said, but there was a distant look in her eyes, which were focused on the river.

"Your sister is pretty and she's a wild child. Sigal. I think she's in trouble."

She gave me a quick glance and then turned back to the river. It's a good thing it was there. She patted her face again. "You think?"

It came from far away, from a place I wasn't familiar with, not the place I thought was reserved for sisters. But what do I know?

The waiter placed my drink in front of me. When he was far enough away, I said, "I think, and I'm almost convinced." Then I added, because it was time, "Let's get things straight between us. I'm here because of your family; I'm guessing your father, contacted our office. I admit I like Bangkok, but I have no other reason to be here at this particular time."

She gazed at me as directly and openly as possible. "Assuming what you say about Sigal is true, what's your first step?"

"The usual. Look, Bangkok is a big city with a long name that no foreigner can even pronounce—Krung Thep Mahanakhon

Amonrattanakosin—and it goes on, for a total of one hundred and sixty-seven letters. Do you think anyone in a city with a name like that gives a damn about one Israeli woman, even if she's pretty? When someone sinks below the surface here, they don't usually pop up again."

She didn't reply, continuing to pat at the perspiration on her neck in silence. Finally, she said, "I don't like the way you choose to paint the picture."

"It's not me," I said. "It's just how things are here. I can understand if you don't want to see it that way."

After a long pause, she gave me a hard look. "I don't know why I'm sitting here having a drink with you," she said.

"Because you thought I might be able to tell you something that would solve the mystery of Sigal's disappearance. Then she'd suddenly show up and fall into your arms and all would be forgotten. But mysteries like this don't get solved with abracadabra and the wave of a magic wand. Sigal is missing. That's a fact. When people go missing in the East, it's generally for one of two reasons: either they want to disappear or someone makes them disappear. Let's hope Sigal falls into the first category, because unfortunately, there's not much we can do in the second case scenario except to look for her and maybe, if we're lucky, we'll find her body."

She leaned forward on her elbows and stared at me. There was no emotion in her eyes. "I know Sigal well enough to know she can take care of herself in any situation."

"And what life experience do you base that on?" I said more sharply than I intended. "Growing up in a large house with a live-in cook and a full-time gardener? Two years in the Army as a secretary? A three-month trip to the East?"

"Don't be cynical, Mr. Naor."

"Call me Dotan," I broke in. "And here's what I'm most curious about at the moment. What are you doing here?"

"Isn't it obvious? I'm here for Sigal."

"You don't have to be here for Sigal. You could just as well have stayed home." As soon as I said "home" I saw a flash of anger in her eyes, but she doused it quickly.

"What do you think she got herself mixed up in?" I asked.

Her deep green eyes gave me the sort of look that says, "I've got your number, mister. Cool it."

"She might have gotten mixed up in something, I don't know what. But that doesn't mean she can't look out for herself."

"Might," I echoed. "I hope you're right, but I'm working on my own assumption, based on considerable experience. I think you're sadly mistaken. If Sigal is still alive, I think she's in some dark, dangerous hole that's not so easy to get out of."

She chose not to listen. "My sister won't be pleased to hear that her father is interfering in her life. She's very cocky and very independent."

How far would Sigal go to get back at her father or her sister? The last thing I wanted was to get drawn into the entangled relations in a dysfunctional family. But I had a job to do, and that was the last principle I still stuck to in my own complicated relations with the world.

"That sounds great at a party in Tel Aviv," I said. "But here it can be a matter of life and death. And I'm not talking metaphorically. They don't play games in Bangkok."

She sat up straighter. "You're very proud of your skill at solving other people's problems. But when it comes to yourself, you seem pretty messed up to me."

"I think you've got it the wrong way around," I answered. "I didn't come here to find myself or fix myself. I get paid for what I do. I assume the money is coming from your father, but frankly, I don't know and I don't give a damn. That's what my partner's for, to move me around like a piece on a checkerboard: up, down, or sideways. Sometimes he makes me jump."

I have to admit she was pushing my buttons. I stood up. "Watch out you don't get a chill. The wind can pick up suddenly," I said, pulling a business card from my wallet. "I'm at the Fontaine. You can always reach me on my cellphone."

She didn't take the card. I put it on the table and left.

*　*　*

When I stepped out of the Oriental Hotel, the sun was already blazing. It was broiling hot. I started down a street crowded with stalls selling overpriced souvenirs. The vendors were taking shelter under colorful umbrellas or deep inside their stalls, coming out only to try and reel in an innocent tourist passing by. I was walking at a leisurely pace. A black Mercedes pulled up alongside me. The window rolled down and a clean-shaven head leaned out. The man had a large tattoo that ran down the back of his neck to a spike-studded dog collar. He addressed me in Hebrew with a heavy Russian accent.

"My name is Ivan. Around here I'm known as Ivan the Durian."

"Pleased to meet you," I said with a laugh, not stopping. "It suits you. Big, prickly, and smelly."

The Mercedes rolled forward, keeping pace with me. It was obvious he didn't share my sense of humor.

"You talk to her sister. What she tell you?"

I kept walking steadily, not answering.

"Mr. Naor," the bald guy said in the same calm tone, wiping his neck with a wet towel the driver handed him. "My boss, Mr. Alex Weiss, want me to tell you that you are now partners, whether you like or not. You both want same thing, for different reasons. My boss, Mr. Alex Weiss, does not offer to share expenses, but maybe he cut you in on profits if you find Sigal Bardon. Mr. Weiss say this very generous offer, especially for him. You know that if you know him better. But not good idea."

The driver handed him another wet towel, a sign the man had been in Bangkok long enough to have adopted some of its customs. He was starting to infuriate me. My anger was rising like cloudy spume. I could have ignored the creep, but there was something oddly satisfying in my repressed rage. I knew where it was coming from, but I didn't want to admit to myself that the meeting at the Oriental didn't end as I had envisioned. What was I hoping for? That we would smile at each other in blissful harmony? That we would look each other in the eye and the world would come alight? That we would hold hands and thank the heavenly spirits for bringing us together? She hadn't been very cooperative even on the professional matter of finding Sigal. She was wary, distant, and concerned for her privacy, and Sigal's as well. Why? Did she know something? Or was she just naturally protective of her family?

The bald guy showed up like dessert at the end of a bad meal. We passed the row of shops under the Oriental. I picked up one of the carved walking sticks with a sharp tip they sell as souvenirs. The car was still rolling forward. I stopped short and held the stick up against it. A deep scratch appeared along the whole length of its black body.

Baldy was appalled. He stuck his head out the window to see what damage I had done to his beloved Mercedes. I could tell I had scarred his prize possession.

"*Blyad*, motherfucker," he blurted. "I get you later."

Ivan the Durian rolled up the dark window and the Mercedes sped away.

* * *

It was time to probe more deeply into Mr. Weiss. I texted Shai in the office: *Send everything you have on Weiss, including pictures.*

Khao San was a ten-minute drive away. I hailed a cab. To my amazement, the driver was totally unknown to me. I got out and went into one of the many internet cafés on the street where I checked my email. Shai had already come through, sending a message with a long list of attachments. One was the scan of a newspaper article with a pyramid-shaped diagram of an Israeli drug cartel whose tentacles reached across Europe and Asia. It contained the names of several well-known underworld figures and their henchmen. One of them was Alex Weiss. I clicked on a photo. His face wasn't particularly memorable, except for the eyes. Small and half-closed, the dark pupils peered out like cold black beads.

"Not a very nice guy," I muttered out loud. I sent the picture to the printer on the counter beside the manager. She was a tiny thing dressed in hot pants and flip-flops. As she pulled the sheet of paper from the printer, she gave it a quick glance. I saw her expression freeze. "You know him?" I asked.

"Yes," she said, looking up at me. "Not good man."

That was enough for me. I fed the photo into the shredder beside the counter, sorry I had printed it out. But it was too late now.

CHAPTER TEN

THINGS QUIET DOWN in the early evening hours. The tourists have finished their sightseeing and shopping for the day and are heading for supper.

Patpong 3 isn't the prettiest street in the world, or even the prettiest in Bangkok. The difference between it and Patpong 1 and 2 is not that they're long and it's short, or that they're lined with shops and here there are only bars with no other distractions. The difference is that Patpong 3 is the street of gays.

Among the bars occupying both sides of the street, homosexuality has never been considered a disease or deviation. They don't talk about it much, but it's a legitimate part of life. Maybe not as legitimate as in Japan in the samurai era, when the only kind of love regarded as worthy of a true warrior was between two men, or in the Buddhist monasteries in China in the ninth and tenth centuries, when monks routinely had relations with their apprentices. But homosexuality is the essence of Patpong 3. Not that it's my thing, but as far as I'm concerned, people can do whatever they want.

From the top of the street I already saw my second passport—Micha Waxman.

He was sitting on a tall stool at one of the bars open to the street. A counter with a few beer taps and pint glasses. A handsome well-built bartender in a short tuxedo jacket and bow tie stood behind it. Two young locals were sitting next to Micha. Another young man came down the street and leaned over to him. They kissed on the mouth with exaggerated sucking noises. I heard Waxman say effeminately in English, "Do you love me, sweetie?"

Laughing, the man continued on to the next bar. The two men sitting with Waxman were totally indifferent. Micha was fresh meat on display, just like them, only paler.

It was my turn.

"Hi," Micha said. The asshole didn't even recognize me.

"Last time I saw you, you weren't in such a sociable mood," I said.

He looked different. Then his skin had been jaundiced and he was a sweaty wreck. Now he was stuffed into skinny jeans that accentuated his package. A black button-down shirt that tapered down to his waist was half open, revealing a smooth chest and the gold hamsa.

I saw him tense up. Tense was good.

He checked the street. "What do you want from me? Who told you I was here?"

The sour odor of his fear reached my nostrils, which widened with a certain pleasure at the familiar smell.

"Shaya, right?" he went on. "That maniac. Give him a little blow and he'll sing like a bird. Israeli shitheads are a dime a dozen. Why are you following me?"

"We have to talk," I said. "I'm glad to see you're looking better. Last time you were wasted."

"You can't just come here and harass me."

"What makes you so sure?"

He scanned the street again. No one was paying any attention to us. They all knew what was going on. The two guys next to him had become extras, like the supporting actors on a Japanese kabuki stage. They didn't exist, not even in their own minds. Waxman was becoming increasingly upset. The insipid smile of the male whore fishing for a client had been wiped from his face.

"People know me here," he said.

"Great. So are we going to have that talk?"

"Come inside. Put your arm around me like you're a client."

I had no intention of doing any such thing. Just the thought of his needle-marked arm and sweaty shoulder, despite the inordinate amount of deodorant he had undoubtedly sprayed on himself, made me sick to my stomach. Very few things put me off, or affect me at all for that matter, but a gay drughead in Bangkok is one of them.

We went into the bar, lit dimly with red bulbs. There was a DJ in the back, a transvestite with a large bosom in a long red kimono and heavy makeup. A few male couples moved on the dance floor. A foreigner with a huge pot belly was wrapped around a local boy with a flat stomach and ass. Two older men, both high, minced around the floor.

"This is how you make your living?" I asked when we were seated at a table in the corner.

"Yeah. So what?"

Without knowing it, I had apparently touched a nerve. Or else it was just his way to elicit sympathy, like every other whore in Bangkok who tells you about the village she came from, the little boy she left behind, and the man who abandoned her in the cruel city to fend for herself. The story is always true, but they only tell it for one purpose: to pry open the client's wallet. Micha Waxman was no different. He started whining.

"You want to hear more? I used to be an actor. Mostly, I played clowns. The theater manager came on to me and in the end, I moved in with him. He was horrible. The meanest fag you've ever met. He used me, humiliated me, made me believe I was worthless, a nothing. After him, the only thing left for me was to sell myself. Once I seduced a flight attendant, another time I undressed a fisherman at the seaside. What brought them to me, what sent them away—what difference does it make? I only did it to earn enough to survive. Money, money, money. That's all there is. Then I came here and did the same thing. It's easy here. Everyone sells themselves. Everyone's a whore."

"Cut the philosophy and self-pity," I said sharply. "Where's Sigal Bardon?"

Telling his story had made him forget his fear. It returned now like a boomerang. He was having trouble breathing.

"I already told you. I have no idea."

"You were the last one to see her."

"I don't know." He looked at the hand I had placed on the table. "What do you want from me?"

"You know what I think?" I said. "I think you're a fucking liar. You went to the train station with Sigal."

"Yeah, so what? I told you, she came to my room. We shot up together. She's worse than I am. Real hard-core."

The past began to rise up in me. I was the old Dotan Naor from the Security Agency. Sweat started running down my arms to my hands, lighting them on fire. I could squash this bug in an instant.

"Where did you meet her?"

"Nowhere in particular. Khao San."

"Liar," I hissed, pressing harder. "If we weren't in a public place, I'd punch you in the face. What was in the duffel bag?"

"How should I know?" He squirmed in his chair in an attempt to distance himself from my fist, which was already clenched.

"Where did she go?"

He was at the stage when he was starting to feel the rug being pulled out from under his feet, the stage when you can't let up. You push harder and harder, keep shoving him into a corner, until you see him break.

"I think you're so stressed out because you're worried about what's going to happen to you because you got involved with Sigal. I bet that after I came to see you yesterday you stuck the needle in as far as it would go and took the biggest hit you could get. Why don't you give yourself a break? Just tell me what happened. I want to know where she is. You read me?"

He started shaking, but this time it wasn't the drugs. "Who are you? What are you getting out of this?"

"I'm a private investigator. Her family's looking for her," I said.

"I'll give you a few thousand bahts. My parents are sending me money tomorrow. I'll get you a free lay, boy or girl, whatever you want. Just leave me alone. I don't know nothing."

Fucking moron. I grabbed him where his neck met his head and pressed down on the muscle. Just a little. Only two fingers. I could have pressed harder, but he wasn't one of those muscle-bound gays. He was scrawny, skin and bones from all the drugs he shot up. Drugs and AIDS have one thing in common—they eat your flesh. So I only applied a little pressure, but it was enough. He started writhing. The barman held his position behind the bar, ignoring us. Those people know when it's best to turn a blind eye. The glasses suddenly needed his full attention. The transvestite DJ put the headphones back on and turned up the music. I increased the pressure slightly.

"You don't want me to hurt you, do you? All I want is the truth."

"What truth?" Waxman said. "Besides, you don't scare me."

I took my hand away. Something had awoken in him. Experience told me it was time to ease off.

"I'm dead inside anyway," he said. "I'm trapped in such a dark hole that even if you hit me, or he does, I won't feel it."

"Who's 'he'? Who are you talking about? Weiss?"

"I'd tell you, but he'd find out, and that would be the end of me."

There was no doubt he was a worm, but he still had a remnant of spine.

"I have your passport," I said.

He laughed wryly. "Keep it. Consider it a gift. As if I'll ever need it again."

I tried another tack. "Don't you want to help Sigal?"

"Don't you understand? You've got it backwards. Anything I say will just make things worse for her. If you find her, he'll find her. It's not just me you're putting in danger. You can't save her. If the people who love her can't save her, how do you think you're going to do it?"

"Who's 'he'? You mean Weiss?"

His hand was shaking. He lit a cigarette, drew in the smoke, and started coughing. "It's too late for me. I'm a lost cause. I'm through talking. I need a hit."

I got up and walked out of the bar.

Another mistake.

* * *

I should have given more credit to whoever he was. After all, I was in Bangkok, not Tel Aviv. It took no more than twenty or twenty-five minutes from the moment I left the bar.

I heard a scream, a long desperate wail of pain. I could tell it came from him. I hadn't gone far, just three bars away near the end of the street. I was sipping on a beer at the French Kiss, a bar frequented by journalists, opportunist adventurers, and mercenaries looking for a war somewhere in Asia that would offer temporary employment. I was standing, leaning on the bar, when I heard it.

I ran back, but I was too late. I went into the bar. The ground floor was empty. The dancers had vanished, along with the DJ. Only the barman was still there, indifferently wiping glasses. He picked up a glass, held it up to the light, and then used the towel on his shoulder to polish the rim. The dance music had been replaced by an eerie silence. The large speakers in the corners faced each other, abandoned. Giving me no more than a brief glance, the barman started hanging the glasses on the rack overhead.

Now I had to decide. Do I go inside to the scene of the crime or do I turn around and leave? The second option was neater, but I knew it would take me farther away from Sigal. How much farther? I had no way of knowing. On the other hand, going in meant saying, "Hello, trouble, here I am." So I went in.

I climbed the stairs. The top floor was decorated in Moroccan style, with tiny mirrors embedded in the roughly

plastered walls, arches, and dark intimate niches closed off by
curtains, the lamps behind them casting a dim, seductive red
light. I pulled aside the first curtain. Then the second. Nothing.
Empty.

He was in the next cubicle, a large space almost entirely occupied by a huge bed, a place for chance encounters of the type
agreed on over a beer or a meaningful look on the dance floor.
Naturally, the establishment provided all the amenities: a
slender barefoot Thai boy to give you a foot massage, a
Cambodian boy with large black eyes who'd been smuggled
across the border for fifty dollars to bring ice-cold beer to you
in bed. For a little extra you could have the boy in your bed as
well. They're very service-oriented in the East. I remembered
the words of Yukio Mishima: "A woman's beauty grows over
time. But the life of a young lad is only a single day in spring,
the day before flowering."

A sweet, heavy odor hung in the air, like the scent of honeysuckle. But Micha Waxman was no flower now. He was lying
facedown on the bed half-covered in silk pajamas, his thigh,
butt, and the crack between the white cheeks exposed. The
dagger was stuck in the left side of his back, up to the hilt, and
the blood had already spilled onto the floor, mixing with the
water left by the small foot massage basin. It was so expected
that I was furious with myself. I moved closer. His right hand
was under his body while his left arm lay on the mattress
bearing the dark red scars of the needle or maybe a recent skin
disease. I leaned over, picked up his hand, and twisted it backwards to open the clenched fist. It worked. For a little while
after death, the body retains its flexibility.

In his hand was a dark business card with orange flames on
both sides. In the middle was the word "Apocalypse."

CHAPTER ELEVEN

THE COPS ARRIVED sooner than I anticipated. I remembered seeing a Tourist Police post on the corner. It was too late to make myself scarce before they showed up, but I hadn't been planning to do that anyway. There were too many people in the street, and too many people had seen me in the bar with Micha.

When the two cops saw me beside the body, they exchanged words quickly, and then one barked, "You, passport."

I took out my passport and handed it over. He passed it to his partner, barking, "You, wall."

I faced the wall and raised my hands slowly. He patted me down in search of concealed weapons. By the time he gestured for me to turn around, the homicide squad was already there. Two young detectives in suits. They surveyed the scene. The tourist cops in their black uniforms bowed. One read out to them from his notebook, speaking in a whisper and throwing me a glance. The detectives nodded and looked at me. The cop bowed again and went back to his partner. They stood at the entrance, barring entry or exit from the cubicle.

An officer marched in. He was built like a tank, nearly as broad as he was tall. His face was flattened like a boxer's and

covered in pockmarks. Standing in front of me, he announced, "I am Major Somnuk." The jab of his two-way radio
in my stomach almost sent my body into shock. I collapsed
onto the floor. He remained standing over me in the same
threatening pose.

His men were pulling the place apart. One was shouting at
a young gay who entered the cubicle, presumably the owner,
periodically reinforcing his words with a slap across the face.
The owner's face got redder with each blow.

I wasn't in much better shape. Slowly, I pulled myself up.
Major Somnuk had large ears with fleshy lobes. I learned a long
time ago that, although ears like that on a statue of Buddha
signify wisdom, on real people they're a sign of an aggressive
temperament, something like an elephant in heat. He gave me
a cold stare, his jaws rhythmically chewing on something.
Probably the last bite of meat from his dinner that he still
hadn't swallowed. There was nothing about him I liked.

"What your story?" he asked. "You friend of him?" He gestured with his thumb toward the bed.

"No, I never saw him before today," I lied, not knowing how
much they knew.

He let out a sound that resembled an "aaah" and gave me a
sharp look. One of the young detectives came over and glanced
at me suspiciously while speaking to his superior. Major
Somnuk listened. Not a single muscle in his face moved.

"My detective tell me you talk to this fellow a little time
ago," he said, pinning me with his dark eyes. "You like queer
bars? You like fuck them, macho *falang*, or you like slaps from
boy with smooth face who make your eye swell up and break
your jaw?" I passed a hand over my face. Were there any marks
left? I wondered if I should say something about my rights as a

tourist, a guest in their country, or if I should tell him I was on the job too. But the way he moved the radio in his hand made it clear to me it would be best to cooperate. Major Somnuk wasn't pulling any punches. His descriptions were very graphic. I felt like asking him how he had acquired his knowledge, but the trick in these situations is to shut up and take it. The opposite works too: take it and shut up. But you have to train yourself to take it. That also teaches you something about ego. Like all experienced interrogators, cops like Major Somnuk know how to squash your ego, how to make you feel smaller than a bug, as small as a microbe.

"I talked to him," I said.

He didn't seem interested in listening, so I shut up. He must have gotten fed up with the piece of meat stuck between his teeth because he spit it out into the corner. His icy eyes were empty. He went over to Micha's body and turned it over slowly, as if he were afraid it might disintegrate. The light from the overhead bulb fell onto the small hamsa hanging from a gold chain around his neck and onto the flesh below the collarbone. Major Somnuk barked something at one of his men who barked something at the cops at the entrance. One of them left and came back dragging a boy by the arm. For the moment, the kid was still as pretty as a red hibiscus the day it blooms, but by the time they got through with him, he'd look like a dried-up leaf. He was dressed in tight shorts and a tank top that revealed the feminine curves of his shoulders. But as I said, in this world, beauty doesn't last long. The cop hauled him over to Major Somnuk and let go. He stood there, cringing, struggling to execute a bow with his hands in front of him in the traditional *wai* gesture.

Somnuk spoke to him in a voice that was unexpectedly soft, gentle, almost paternal. It came from a culture long familiar with flesh of every variety. The boy began to answer in Thai, but Somnuk cut him off. "Speak English so *falang* understand."

When the boy raised his eyes to me, his expression gave me an eerie sensation. It conveyed total acceptance of his plight, developed over years of experience. There was no need to guess his life story; it was written on his face. He gave me a long look. "Not him," he said finally. "The *falang* big like him," he said, pointing to me, "but fat and no hair, like egg."

Somnuk looked disappointed. The police in Thailand have a propensity to close cases quickly, too quickly. It might work with local goons, but foreigners are a headache. So they prefer to lock them up first and investigate later. It's more than likely that by the time the legal process kicks in, they'll confess, or maybe cut their wrists with a rusty razor blade or shoot up with a used needle and get AIDS. If that happens, they'll go quickly for lack of treatment and a compromised immune system. There's also the possibility that the unfamiliar surroundings and uncertainty about their future will send them around the bend, so when their consular agent finally shows up there won't be anything left of them worth bothering with.

"So what your connection with him?" Major Somnuk asked me, gesturing with his radio toward Waxman's body. It was the first question he didn't bark at me. Not that I imagined his Buddhist compassion was starting to show. I knew I shouldn't count on the likelihood of his having spent three months in a monastery as a child, a common practice in his country, where he might have soaked up a measure of humanity. But since my gut was still hurting, I decided to be more accommodating.

There was no doubt in my mind that he was annoyed at being called away from dinner at his favorite club, where scantily dressed girls had been serving him bowls of savory meat. He was probably getting a foot massage while he ate.

"I was trying to help a kid out. Yesterday a cab driver gave me his passport and told me where to find him," I said, reaching for the back pocket of my jeans. I stopped short when I saw the sharp look in Somnuk's eyes. His hand moved toward the gun holstered on his waist. I wasn't in America, but cops in Thailand don't like their suspects to make sudden movements either.

"I'm unarmed," I said. "I'm going to take the passport out of my pocket very slowly." I reached behind me, moving as slow as I could, but my brain was running a sprint. I knew luck had to be on my side. I needed the best karma in the world for the passport I pulled out to be Micha's and not Sigal's. They weren't any different to the touch, so there was nothing I could do to further my cause except maintain the most composed façade I could manage. I turned the expression off in my eyes, shut down my emotions, eased out one of the passports, and handed it to him.

Major Somnuk's lieutenant took it from me and examined the photo, comparing it with the face of Micha Waxman on the bed. Apparently, there was still enough similarity between them to satisfy him. I took a deep breath. "I went looking for him, to give him back his passport, but he was too strung out. He didn't care. He didn't even want it."

"That best story you can give me?" Somnuk asked.

I didn't answer.

"You fuck him before you stick knife in his back?" His tone made it seem like a normal question, the kind he asked as a matter of routine. Maybe it was. Or maybe it was his own private fantasy. Or not a fantasy at all. I remembered Tom and his preference for ladyboys. He once told me that after the operation, what used to be their penis becomes part of a vagina that's so sensitive their orgasms drive them wild.

"Do I look like a murderer?" I asked.

"Anyone can be murderer," he answered. "In Bangkok people change. Everything very cheap, whores, drugs, so people look for blood."

I didn't know if he was referring to locals or foreigners, or whether they were all the same to him. But I did know what he meant. Bangkok represents unlimited freedom. Anything's possible. The kingdom tolerates all forms of deviants. You can do whatever you want, just as long as you don't insult the king or the Buddhist establishment. But Major Somnuk didn't like foreigners. And I knew he wasn't going to make my life easy.

"What hotel you at?" he asked.

"The Fontaine."

My answer drew a laugh from Somnuk and his lieutenant. "You like be close to action. Don't want waste time," he said, adding with a threat in his voice, "You stay where we can find you."

* * *

After seeing the body of Micha Waxman, the only thing in my mind on the way back to the hotel was a long shower. What had happened in the twenty minutes after I left him? The place where the body was found indicated he was expecting a long night of lovemaking, but with whom? Someone he knew? A regular? Someone who had tempted him with a wink

and a whisper to go upstairs and then left him to die an ago-
nizing death? There wasn't the slightest doubt in my mind
that his death had something to do with Sigal. I remembered
the last thing he said to me: If the people who love her can't
save her, how could I? What did he mean? He was obviously
afraid of Alex Weiss, and I still had to find out why, but at the
end he was talking about someone else. Someone who loved
Sigal but couldn't save her. Who? For a while I'd sensed a
shadow operating in the background, but now its presence
was becoming more real.

Hotel rooms are supposed to be locked, but the door to
mine was ajar. Inside it looked very different from the way I'd
left it, and certainly very different from the way it should have
looked after maid service had been there. The few clothes I'd
brought with me were lying in a pile on the rug. My suitcase
was upside down, open like an oyster after the meat has been
extracted. The lining had been slashed. But luggage can't complain. A tie was hanging from the floor lamp as if someone was
mocking my taste. That always irritates me—disguised
mockery that doesn't give you a chance to respond.

What were they looking for? The passports? I only had one
left, Sigal's, and that was in my pocket. Major Somnuk had
taken Micha's. But it didn't seem likely that's what they were
after. So what was it? And who was it? Cops sent by Somnuk,
or Weiss's guys? Not that I saw a big difference between them
at this point.

I had the unpleasant feeling that instead of being on Sigal's
trail, I was being led by the nose down some other path and
I had no idea where it was taking me. Things couldn't go
on like this much longer. Something had to happen. One way
or another.

I went out to the hallway. Two men stepped out of a room. Obviously, Israelis.

"Did you see anyone go into my room?" I asked.

"Why? Did someone break in?" the older one asked.

"Bastards," the younger one said. "Come on, we'll buy you a drink. Forget about it. This is Bangkok. They have no respect for anyone here, and there's no one to talk to either. What can you do about it? Go to the cops?"

I thanked them for the invitation and said I'd take a rain check. Then I went downstairs. The young man behind the reception desk was dripping with smiles until I told him what had happened. He dialed a number, presumably maid service, and I watched as his expression turned to dismay. Then he apologized that anything like that could have happened at their hotel and promised that someone would tidy the room immediately. Meanwhile, he offered me coffee on the house.

I thanked him and declined the offer.

"Do you want me to call the police?" he asked.

I'd had enough cops for one day. I told him not to bother, although I knew that the moment I turned my back he'd make the call. It was his duty to report it. And it was safe to assume that anyone working hotel reception was a police informant.

I went back to my room thinking it was time to get things straight in my head. Surprisingly, the bottle of Jameson had been left untouched. I unscrewed the cap and took a long drink. There were three things I was certain of. Each of them bugged me and all three together really pissed me off. I took another swig. Someone had been playing me from the second I set foot in Bangkok. Another swig. Micha Waxman had been murdered. The next time I pulled on the bottle, I could see the bottom, and that really made me mad. I was convinced there was a connection between Micha's murder, Sigal, and Weiss. The only thing left to find out was who was pulling the strings. But the bottle was empty.

I couldn't stay there anymore. I left the clothes where they were, taking only my toothbrush and razor. There aren't many things, or even people, I'm attached to, but those two items have accompanied me down many long roads.

CHAPTER TWELVE

KHAO SAN ROAD, in the Banglamphu district, has earned itself a reputation worldwide. It's not particularly long, but it's wider than most streets in Bangkok. At night, the street-long bazaar, where stall-holders hawk clothes, flip-flops, silver jewelry, used books, and other items popular with backpackers, becomes of secondary interest. The crowds stream in and the road fills with young Western males with voracious eyes, Western girls who sat for hours in the sun getting their hair braided and now want to feel alive, exhausted waitresses who have already been dragging their feet for hours but have to keep at it if they don't want to be fired by the Chinese café owner, girls in neon colors handing out flyers for night clubs and calling out the prices of the drinks—"Singha beer just 100 bahts, Heineken beer *sem sem*," the familiar phrase for "fixed price" aimed at drawing in the young Western *falangs*. Everyone knows they're loaded despite their scruffy appearance.

I was halfway down the street when I heard the rumbling sound of motorcycles behind me. I turned and watched as they came closer. Three motorcycles racing through the crowds, wildly spurting ahead and braking suddenly, sending the pedestrians running for safety.

Why did I have the feeling they were coming for me? New 125cc Hondas, the most popular model in Bangkok. Hundreds of motorbike taxis just like them waited on every corner. The three drivers were clad in black leather jackets, the dark visors of their helmets hiding their faces. But I didn't have to see them to identify them. I knew exactly who they were: the boxers from the alley. Apparently, they weren't just random street thugs who'd been given a thousand bahts to harass me. Whoever was after me was raising the ante. They had come to do more than simply deliver a message.

I'm not wet behind the ears. Haven't been for years. I've got a very firm stance and enough weight to land a serious punch. I made my body as loose as possible, assuming they were aiming to get within kicking distance of me. Unless, of course, they were planning to stab me. It's no problem for an experienced motorcyclist to let go of the handlebars long enough to knife someone without even slowing down. The way they were riding, they looked very experienced, as if they'd grown up on two wheels. They sped up. The first two passed me, grazing me on purpose. The third stopped beside me, his tires squealing. He raised the visor with a gloved hand, revealing a broad face and slightly slanted eyes. There was nothing special about the punk aside from a large dark mole beside his nose. "Go home, *falang*," he said. "Next time you're dead." Then he leaned on the gas and took off.

"The people here are crazy," said a passing American guy with long hair and two young ladies on his arms, one American and one local. I nodded and kept walking.

Up ahead of me was a familiar figure, a woman I hadn't seen in a long time: Mama Dom. Her fat idiot son was with her. How long had it been since I saw her last? Three, four years? Maybe more. I'd been robbed like a country bumpkin. Pretty girl, motel. The next day, Mama Dom showed up with my wallet. Nothing had been taken. She pulled a thousand-baht note from it and said in broken English, "It for my expenses. We not want trouble with foreign police." Then she disappeared.

I wondered what she was doing here now. It was no accident. Mama Dom is a crime boss, although you couldn't tell by looking at her. To the uninitiated she looks like a homeless woman as she drags her feet from one stall to the next collecting her weekly protection money. Half the stalls on Khao San belong to her. She's into everything illegal: betting; cock fights in back alleys; drugs, particularly ya ba, the tablets that fuck with the heads of half of Bangkok's slum population; prescription drugs; fake passports—you name it. I've seen her in action: a frowsy old lady who can turn into a venom-spitting cobra. If she was here, something must be going on.

It was.

She turned and started walking toward me. I pretended not to recognize her, but Mama Dom never forgets. Not anything. She hoards it all: information, memories, rags. Her restless little pig eyes caught me. She stopped, smiled to reveal teeth that were reddish black from all the betel quid she chewed, and gestured for me to follow her.

Nothing happens in Bangkok's main streets except for traffic jams and car accidents. Anything of any consequence takes place in the side streets, the *sois*, to which the Thais have brought their village life. There, young men on motorcycles and high on speed still show respect to their elders. There, young girls from the Isan district in the northeast, who were sold into prostitution for a sack of rice, still bring gifts to the

Buddha in the neighborhood temple. There, order reigns, and a person is esteemed according to their station. Mama Dom occupies a very high station.

She was waiting for me. She took out a bag with Coke, ice, and a straw and gave it to her son to suck on to silence the grunts he uttered constantly as she towed him along behind her wherever she went. He sat down on the sidewalk on a small piece of cardboard she laid out for him. A woman in a straw hat behind the steaming pots in a nearby stall brought out a yellow plastic chair for her to sit on.

Mama Dom's English was minimal, like that of your average street whore, consisting mainly of a lot of fucky-fucky and boom-boom. But this time she made herself surprisingly clear. "You give me five hundred green, I tell you where *falang* lady."

"What lady?" I asked.

Giving me no more than a brief glance, Mama Dom got up. She smacked the plastic bag out of her son's hand and walked away, dragging him wailing behind her.

"Khun Mama Dom," I called, adopting a more respectful approach.

She turned, looking at me as if to say, What? Now you're trying to suck up to me? Get me the money. You know how the game is played in Bangkok. First the money. Then she stopped and said coldly, "Israel *falang* think Thai people see money only. Thai people think money to show they serious. *Falang* talk-talk about everything, also about money. In end they close hand like bunker. Who care what *falang* talk? *Falang* talk like duck ass in water. Only open and close. Talk not worth nothing and *falang* not learn nothing. So how *falang* want to find what *falang* look for?"

I kept silent. That's one thing you learn in the East. You never know when you'll get a sermon or a punch in the nose. And you never know who you will get it from. "*Falang* not understand karma," Mama Dom went on. "*Falang* lady live or dead. It same."

"Khun Mama Dom," I said. "The *falang* lady has a mother, a father. Maybe she made a mistake. *Mai pen rai*—it doesn't matter."

"*Falang* talk like idiot. Boring. No mistake. Karma. Karma only law. *Falang* think he better. *Falang* talk justice, morals. Piss me off. When mosquito bite at night, it hard to sleep. When water buffalo fly look for place to put eggs, it sting. Hurt all day. When *falang* lady run, she pay. No talk about it."

"Why did she run?" I asked.

The look in her eyes was contemptuous. Her son was still wailing. She said something to the woman in the stall, who was frying rice noodles and sprouts. The lady left her pan and got a bottle of Coke from the refrigerator. Mama Dom handed it to him.

"*Falang* like my son," she said. "No think."

Again, I kept silent.

Gazing at me, she said, "*Falang* no talk. That good."

I remained silent. What could I say? I saw the sparkle in her eyes. She was enjoying every minute.

"Where *falang* go sleep?" she asked. "No can return to hotel."

They know everything here, I thought to myself. If Mama Dom knew, everyone did. No one was talking, but someone was calling the shots. I was the only one still in the dark.

"Come," she said. "Mama Dom find you place bon-bon. Major Somnuk not know. Mr. Weiss not know."

She took the bottle from her son. Naturally, he started wailing, but he trailed after her. I followed. We made a rather strange procession, but no one ever looks at Mama Dom. Because she knows and never forgets. Not anything.

We walked in the direction of the Banglamphur temple. Behind the monks' cabins was a small one-story building. Several doors faced the alley. Three giggling girls were rinsing vegetables with a hose and cleaning offal in blue plastic basins, making supper for the women in Mama Dom's little whorehouse. She kept going. We came to a large warehouse where a few children were sitting on the floor sorting plastic parts from old radios and computers for recycling. In the back was a door.

Mama Dom opened it with a flourish. The room was simple, almost spartan. A bed with a thin flowery spread, a straw chair, a plywood closet, and a corner shower behind a curtain even more flowery than the bedspread.

"You pay two hundred bahts for night. It okay," she said. "It not Fontaine Hotel but no one know you here."

I said the only thing I could. Thank you.

She was already at the door when she turned and said, "You look for Israel *falang*. In Krung Thep long time."

"Who are you talking about?" I asked.

"Angel for all Israel *falang*," she said, and walked out.

I'd gotten something more than just a room. In fact, I'd gotten quite a lot, although I didn't yet know how much. All I knew was that at some stage I'd have to pay. Mama Dom didn't give anything away for free.

CHAPTER THIRTEEN

I WAS IN urgent need of a cold beer.

I settled myself on a stool at a bar opposite the entrance to the Apocalypse Club. If Micha and Sigal had been in any of the establishments around here, this would be the one. The street was crowded with pedestrians. I was drinking Singha straight from the bottle when I felt someone press up against me. The guy was slovenly and unkempt, his hair twisted into a mass of tangled dreadlocks tied back with a filthy rag. I could smell his hair from miles away. A rolled-up woolen blanket hung by a rope from his shoulder. "Hey, bro," he said in Hebrew, "buy me a beer?"

Strung out or otherwise, he had identified me as Israeli.

"Why should I?" I asked. The piece of human shit had striking black eyes. They were the only thing about him that was clean.

"Around here they believe that if you give to the monks, you'll be rich in the next life, if you buy a poor man a beer, you'll find love in this life. It's all about racking up karma points." I laughed, gesturing to the young waitress in a yellow T-shirt to bring another bottle. He held it up to his mouth and took a long drink. His hand was shaking, but there was the sign of a good upbringing in the way he said, "Thanks, bro."

Two young punks walked by and opened their foul mouths. "Hey, Valium. You find yourself a sucker?" Instantly, his distant smile disappeared, along with the longing for a different life that I thought I'd glimpsed in his eyes. All that was left was bile. "What's it to you?" he shot back.

"Why 'Valium'?" I asked.

"That's what they call me. I can't remember my real name. It's the Datura. I get these headaches. Agony. Then I scream for Valium. It's the only thing that helps." With a laugh, he added, "It's also the only thing I can get without a prescription. So everyone calls me Valium."

Moonflower, Datura innoxia, I thought. He was another victim of the plant with the innocent-looking white bell-shaped flowers that contain alkaloids from the atropine family, a poison that causes hallucinations and can be lethal if not used properly. Not long ago I found Yoav, an Israeli kid whose memory was erased by a few drops extracted from a Datura plant. The sadhus in India, holy men who have renounced the material world in search of more profound meaning, take it to induce the deepest meditative state. Two or three drops and they can cross the boundaries of consciousness into the depths of the soul, into a madness where they wander through the infinity of the incomprehensible. You have to be a very stupid *falang* to imagine you can handle something the sadhus have learned to control over thousands of years of meditation, hallucinations, delirium, and asceticism. All I could do for him was ask, "Another beer, Valium?"

"Sure," he said, with a crafty look in his eyes. What an elementary existence, I thought. "That club across the street, who owns it?" I asked. I was hoping it was only his long-term memory that had been wiped out.

"Weiss," he said. "The man's got bucks and balls. He hit it big. Used to date one of the top models in Thailand. He's got connections all over. Everyone knows him."

"Can I get H around here?" I asked.

Valium was getting excited. He could already see this was going to pay off. "Just H? I can get you anything you want. China White, ecstasy, speed, opium, ganja, Buddha stick. Just say the word."

"Is Weiss in charge of the transport?"

He started laughing like a madman. "My dad was in charge of transport for the electric company." He laughed hysterically, and then stopped abruptly. Apparently, he still had a trace of common sense. "I don't know," he mumbled.

Israelis control one of the trafficking routes for hard drugs in the East. I'm not talking about backpackers hoping to make it rich by doing a little amateur smuggling. I'm talking about real crime syndicates. I've heard from several sources that merely transporting the drugs isn't enough for them anymore. Their appetite has grown. They want to get into production too, become partners in the opium fields in Laos. And I knew that an agent of one of the biggest syndicates had been in Bangkok, negotiating with Myanmar's military junta over construction of a plant to manufacture ya ba, the "crazy pill" that's the drug of choice in Thailand. Was Sigal's disappearance connected in some way to the drug lords? At this stage, I was working on the assumption that it was, but I still didn't know how or how directly. What had she done that set their food chain on fire? And what link was Weiss in that chain? Micha Waxman's murder was proof that the people involved weren't just little fish. I had no doubt that a lot of drugs, and a lot of money, were on the line.

It was time to leave. I gestured for Valium to get lost. His years of living on the streets told him he wasn't going to get any more out of me. The road to Nirvana is paved with obstacles. The beers I'd bought him were the most he could hope for, and he knew the time had come to move on. I realized I wasn't much different from him. I, too, was feeding off the morsels of information and half-uttered remarks I managed to squeeze out of the people I came into contact with in Bangkok. It's a lousy feeling to know that everyone else is smarter than you. I had to kick it up a gear.

CHAPTER FOURTEEN

I CROSSED THE street to the club. "Cross" isn't really the right word. I cut a path through the sea of excited, sweaty, sticky humanity on the prowl for a good time. They were all hunting desperately for a place where they could forget who and what they were, where their whole being would become no more than the animalistic drive for lust and gratification, where the only way to cool down was to take the ice cubes from your whiskey glass and press them to your burning face, or to the face of the person beside you, with his or her seductive smile, shiny white teeth, and soft skin.

The doorman was tall and thin, with a crooked nose that must have been broken at some point. Even though his uniform was a little loose, I could imagine the flexible muscles underneath, the long arms with the gloved hands that could easily shove an opponent into a corner, the feet planted firmly on the mat and then rising to kick the other man in the chest or stretch out unexpectedly to trip him up while his elbow, his ultimate weapon, struck him in the side.

I showed him the card I had extracted from Micha Waxman's hand.

He threw me a quick look. "Israeli?"

I nodded.

Staring at the card, he asked, "You been here before?"

"No."

A dark-complexioned kid adorned with leather straps and silver chains appeared beside me. The doorman waved him off. "I don't let his type in," he said. "They're usually good kids until the DJ happens to put their favorite music on, and then all hell breaks loose."

I nodded as if I understood what he was talking about. "Tell me," I said, "the names Sigal Bardon and Micha Waxman mean anything to you?"

It didn't take a prophet to know what his answer would be. "As one Israeli to another, if you're smart, you won't ask me questions like that. I don't want to be impolite and refuse to answer."

I looked at him curiously and then remembered. "I know you. You're a boxer, right?"

Even the most modest people in the world fall into that trap. Oh, Buddha, how wise you were to speak of ego. It's such a basic drive it even tripped up Freud.

"Don't screw with me," he said in a tone of contempt that couldn't hide the pride. "Everyone here knows I was world champion."

"But they weren't all in your boxing class precisely four years ago last September," I said.

He glowed. It's so easy to make people happy. You just have to want to.

"Hey, you're from the Security Agency? Sorry," he apologized, looking around as if he wasn't sure he was allowed to say the name out loud. "It was a pleasure to work with you guys."

I nodded, but he didn't see it. His attention had been drawn to a black limousine making its way through the crowd. It pulled up in front of the club. The driver in a cap and white gloves jumped out and opened the door. A heavyset man with a large bald head and two exceptionally hot local whores got out of the back and headed for the door. He was dressed in a white shirt and a black Armani jacket, the real thing, not a knockoff you can get for two thousand bahts at Patpong market. A dozen gold chains with amulets, bracelets of every shape and color, tight black leather pants, and alligator shoes completed the outfit.

The doorman became a paragon of obsequiousness, proving that muscles and world championships are not everything in our transient, material world.

"How are you tonight, Mr. Weiss?"

"Great, great," Weiss answered, going inside and leaving behind a wake of aftershave as strong as your average tsunami. He glanced at me briefly as he passed, but didn't stop. The piece of shit sent Ivan the Durian to take care of me, I thought, and now he's ignoring me. My picture had undoubtedly come up on one of the links he clicked on when he Googled me. It doesn't take more than two minutes on the net to attach a photo to a name. If he was ignoring me, he must have a reason.

Noticing my expression, the doorman said, "Don't look at me like that. Even a world champion can't make a living from boxing." He waved away another stray trying to get in and smiled broadly at a dark curly-headed Israeli, the type that always looks unshaven, who was also flanked by two hot chicks. His were blonds. "Hey, Avishai. What's up?"

"All good," Curly answered, moving his right hand lower until it was crawling up under the miniskirt on one of the blonds. Her cold blue eyes were hazy from all the speed he'd pumped into her. You could actually smell how impatient he was to get her onto the dance floor and light her up. When she was high as a kite, he'd shove her into the dark restroom in the back for a quickie.

"Give an Israeli a week in Bangkok and he thinks he runs the place," the doorman said, watching enviously as Curly and his girls went inside. Getting a grip on himself, he added, "We work our asses off for years, climb into the ring every week, and what comes of it? Muscle for hire. And that schmuck? He just shows up and he's already popping over to Laos and Cambodia, and each time he comes back he's got a bigger smile and a bigger gold hamsa on his chest, flaunting it." I heard the bitterness of a boxer well past his prime who still had to get into the ring. There would always be young wannabes who didn't mind getting kicked around as long as their names appeared on the fight list of the Lumpini Boxing Stadium, published every Wednesday in the English-language *Bangkok Post*. Something to send home to Mommy on the kibbutz outside Ashkelon, in Paisley near Glasgow, or in one of the projects on the outskirts of Moscow.

"Now you know you can trust me," I said, "so tell me: Does the name Sigal Bardon mean anything to you?"

He focused on the sidewalk across the street. Then he came back to me, colder than ever. "Did she work here? If she was a waitress, I wouldn't know. The turnover is astronomical. They come hoping to hit the jackpot, and then disappear."

"What about Micha Waxman?"

"Look, man, you don't know what you're getting into. We're not back home. No one here is your best bud. Don't you get it yet? Every Israeli in Bangkok is only out for himself. Back off. Let it go while you still can."

It was time to pick him up and shake him a little, like a boxer who falls to the mat and comes to in the middle of the countdown. His trainer has to pour a bucket of ice water on him to wake him up enough to get one more three-minute round out of him.

I waved the Apocalypse Club card in his face. "I got this out of the hand of what was left of Micha Waxman after someone stuck a knife in his back," I said.

I expected the shock treatment to produce results, at least get me a little something to go on. But my boxer friend scanned the area, looking hard behind him at the entrance to the club, before saying, "I don't know nothing. The only thing I can do for you is get you in free. You interested?"

Inside, it was nothing out of the ordinary. Black walls, dim lighting, long bar. Despite the early hour, quite a few males and females were already hanging out, all occupied in the same activity, drinking and checking each other out, and all with the same goal: not to end up alone when the night was over. Loneliness is ugly. I spend a good part of my nights alone and I know exactly what it looks like. We're all on a quest for our soul mate, if not forever then at least for a night or an hour. Each of those time periods has a set price in Bangkok.

I leaned over to the bartender. Judging by her G-string and tiny bra, she also did duty as one of the go-go dancers who worked the aluminum pole in the middle of the dance floor. I ordered a beer, shouting to make myself heard, and she placed a cold bottle of Singha in front of me. I took a sip and then turned to survey my surroundings.

Weiss was sitting in a corner that gave him a view of every-thing going on. A square bottle of whiskey and an ice bucket sat on the table in front of him. The two hot chicks, one on each side, were wrapped around him. Ivan sat a seat away, his eyes glued on Weiss. From time to time he got up and slipped another ice cube in the boss's glass. Each time, Weiss took a sip and went on watching the people crowded into his club.

All of a sudden, I caught sight of Reut Bardon, no less, heading in his direction. What was she doing here? That woman was always up to something. How did she find out about this place?

I moved nearer. Reut had almost reached Weiss when a short, broad-faced man with a large mole beside his nose appeared out of nowhere and blocked her path. Weiss signaled for him to let her by.

Aha, I thought, things are starting to fall into place. Weiss, the man of bucks and balls. The goon with the mole. Oh, yes. I slid to the far end of the bar, as close as I could get to Weiss's table. Ivan had his back to me. I hadn't yet had the pleasure of meeting Weiss in person. As far as I was concerned, everything was cool.

Reut opened her mouth. "I—" she started, but Weiss cut her off abruptly.

"I know who you are," he said. "You're here to screw with me. Sit down."

Reut sat directly opposite him. Weiss gave her an icy look and pointed to the girl on his right. "You know who she is?" he asked.

Reut shook her head.

The girl grasped Weiss's hand and placed it between her legs. "This is Miss Joy," he said. "She's number one in Bangkok. She's got a college degree."

He gave her time to rub herself with his hand before freeing it and pointing to the other girl. "What about her? Any idea who she is?"

Reut didn't answer.

"This one is Miss Chong Nung. First Class." He stroked the bare leg of Miss First Class, who giggled in response.

"You see what kind of life I have?"

Reut kept silent. Without warning, Weiss raised the ice bucket and brought it down hard on the table. The ice cubes flew in the air and the water spilled out. The two girls flinched, but Weiss ignored them. He was consumed by rage.

"So tell me," he said, rising and leaning over the table toward Reut, "why shouldn't I enjoy it? What am I, some kind of fucked-up Buddhist? I'm supposed to suffer? All because your sister fucked me?"

Blanching, Reut started to get up, but the guy with the mole appeared out of the shadows and pushed her down. I left my beer on the bar and braced myself for action.

Weiss's former smugness had drained from his face. He leaned over Reut, furious. "*Idi nahui,* fuck off. You get the message?" His face was bright red. "If there's one thing Alex Weiss won't tolerate, it's being screwed with. Your sister is this small, this small," he repeated, forming a tiny space between his forefinger and thumb and shoving it in Reut's face. His bracelets jangled while the talismans on his gold chain struck the table, nearly overturning his glass. "Bangkok is a small world," he said. "I'll find her." Thrusting his face in hers, he lowered his voice. I could no longer hear him clearly. All I caught was, "Even . . . save her, I'll find her." Or something like that.

Shit, I fumed. I missed the name.

Weiss pulled himself erect. "You'll never see your sister again. Trust me on that," he said. "Now get the fuck outta here."

Reut stood up quickly.

"Get the fuck outta here," Weiss repeated, shrieking.

Reut retreated toward the bar. I went up to her and took her arm gently. She jumped. "You startled me," she said when she recognized me.

Even in the dim light I could see how pale she was. Her red lipstick emphasized her large eyes and their amazing deep green color. Those eyes were now flitting warily from side to side, making sure there were no more surprises in store for her.

"I need some air," she said. "We'll talk outside."

Taking my hand, she led me out of the club.

I hoped Weiss was watching. I'm six feet one, after all, so I'm hard to miss. But the club was dark and smoky and very crowded. Wherever we turned, we rubbed up against frenzied dancers. I caught a glimpse of Weiss. The two girls were again smeared all over him like lipstick.

CHAPTER FIFTEEN

OUTSIDE, THE AIR was thick and fetid, a pungent mix of nocturnal vapors, exhaust fumes, and frying squid. The end-of-day activities were in full swing. Vendors were packing up their wares and then pushing their carts homeward, their heads inclined and the muscles in their outstretched arms bulging with the effort. One by one, they vanished into the infinite abyss that is Bangkok.

Fruit sellers stood on every corner, hoping to dispose of the last of their produce before the morning sun melted the ice. At this time of night, none of the people emerging from the clubs would notice the generous sprinkling of sugar on the pineapple or papaya they bit into. A little sugar at this hour would be welcome, invigorating the blood that had soaked up untold quantities of alcohol and drugs, reducing them to a white funk. Reut and I stopped at a fruit stand, filling a bag with slices of tart green mango. I couldn't take my eyes off her. She was too beautiful for this place, too beautiful to be embroiled in the sinister reality we found ourselves in.

"What did he say to you?" I asked. "I only heard part of it. I wasn't close enough to catch it all."

I wanted to hear her voice, wanted her to talk. At that moment in time, it didn't matter what she said. I realized that if she weren't Sigal's sister, I could easily forget the whole thing, just file it away as another unsolved case. There are plenty of those. We never guarantee success. You start out on an investigation with hope, but things don't always go the way you want. It's the same in life, no?

"All I found out is that Sigal is in danger." She sounded tired, drained. "You were right."

I didn't reply. The worst thing you can say in this sort of situation is, "I told you so."

"He said she owed him money."

"How much?"

"A hundred thousand dollars."

I let out a whistle. "That's serious money," I said. I wanted to ask her again what Weiss had told her, whose name he had mentioned. But I didn't. In retrospect, I think maybe I didn't really want to know. Not then, at least.

What had Sigal gotten herself mixed up in? A hundred thousand dollars is a lot of money anywhere in the world. Here you can get a bullet in the head for much less. The owner of a guesthouse in the north murdered an Israeli backpacker for two thousand dollars. He followed him up a mountain footpath, shot him, and took his passport, camera, and money. Two thousand dollars. It was months before the body was found. The kid had a bullet in the back of the head. The locals all knew who had done it, but no one talked. A hundred thousand dollars wouldn't lead to a single body. That much cash would pave a trail of bodies. And a hundred thousand dollars wasn't a duffel bag filled with weed, either. It was much more serious. I did the math. Such a large sum of money could only mean heroin. It was transported from Shan State in northern Myanmar to northern Thailand, and from there to Bangkok. If, like most smugglers, Sigal was carrying bricks of heroin in sealed wrappers, the kind known as Double Lion because of the image on the logo, she could fit about thirty into a duffel bag. Assuming that each brick weighed about seven hundred grams, we were talking twenty-one K of the finest heroin available. If she got on a train, she was probably heading for Rayong in the south, a main stop on the southern smuggling route to Malaysia. As a mule, she could earn two hundred and fifty a brick, for a total of seven thousand five hundred dollars.

Unless . . .

Unless she disappeared on purpose, taking the bag with her. If that's what happened, she had done the unthinkable. It was no wonder she had lit a fire under the whole of Bangkok. A lot of people now owed a lot of money to a lot of other people.

"He told me she has to return the package," Reut said. "Or else he wants his money back. If he can't get it from Sigal, he'll get it from me." She sounded frightened. With good reason.

I didn't like it that Weiss had threatened her. It meant he was in a corner, under pressure. Whether he had promised to supply the heroin or had already paid for it, without it he was in deep shit. I decided to keep the fact that Reut's life was in danger to myself. I didn't think Weiss would hurt her, at least not at this stage when he still had a chance of finding Sigal and her duffel bag.

A large part of investigative work is this kind of brain work. You turn things over in your mind again and again, consider the options, and see what you're left with. What I still had to figure out was how Sigal had gotten involved in something this big. Backpackers generally smuggle small quantities, usually for their own use. It took organized syndicates to move such a large amount, and they used locals. Did someone hook Sigal up with Weiss? There was another possibility, too: someone was planning to steal the shipment out from under Weiss's nose and keep the profit for themselves, and Sigal was in on it from the beginning. A scheme like that would take humongous balls.

Valium with his filthy dreadlocks suddenly showed up, his head hanging low as usual. "Hey, bro, buy me a beer? I could really use one."

"You always hit on the same sucker twice?" I asked. Raising his eyes, he looked directly at me for the first time. "Sorry, bro. All I see in front of me is the bottle." Then he noticed Reut, and we both saw the confusion come over his face. "But . . . what're you doing here? Shiva Dharma, god of ganja, I'm seeing double."

We stood there in puzzled silence for a moment until it registered. I'd seen the family resemblance between Reut and Sigal's passport picture, but until now, I hadn't realized how strong it was. "How much are you and your sister alike?" I asked her. "In appearance, I mean." Now it was Reut's turn to look confused. "We're sometimes mistaken for each other," she said, "but she's prettier." There was more than a trace of envy in her voice. The older sister had done all the hard work, and then her younger sibling had come along and reaped the rewards.

Valium was already moving off. I ran after him.

"Where did you see her?" I asked him.

"See who?" His brain was becoming befuddled again. I knew I'd lose him soon. By the time the sun came up, his mind would be totally in the dark. I didn't have much time.

"Her," I said, pointing to Reut.

"With Achan Phra Pavana in the temple across the river. Where we sleep."

"Take us there," I said.

He smelled an opportunity. Coaxing like a child, he said, "Buy me a beer, bro, and we'll talk about it."

We were standing in front of a bar. I signaled to the waitress who brought me two bottles of ice-cold Singha. I handed him one and held on to the other. "You'll get this one on the way," I told him.

The three of us started walking toward the top of Khao San Road. In this last hour of darkness, youngsters, drunk or stoned, were sitting on the curb, getting ready to welcome the dawn by sipping on the dregs of a bottle or rolling a joint with a shaky hand. The street sweepers with their large straw hats and primitive brooms would soon arrive. The dust they raised would send the kids back under their sweaty sheets in guest-houses with thin moldy walls. At the corner, cabs were waiting for the nighttime stragglers. We climbed into a cab and made the short ride to the river, getting out at one of the ferry stations along the bank.

In the early hours of the morning, the Chao Phraya is a living history of trade as it was once conducted. Heavily laden boats and barges busily unload produce brought to the city markets from the fertile plains: coconuts from Nakhon Pathom, orchids from the region of Ayutthaya, dried fish from Lopburi. All the colors, odors, and sounds of Thailand. A large ferry slowly made its way to the bank, tying up against the pier. Aside from us, the only passengers were a few elderly monks whose orange robes flapped gently in the morning breeze. Hyacinths bobbed on the water, floating in the opposite direction. Valium took a seat on one of the wooden benches, holding the empty beer bottle and staring at the foamy wake behind the boat.

I handed him the second bottle. He drank it like a hot cup of morning coffee, taking small, measured sips. Reut and I leaned on the metal railing, our arms brushing against each other.

"It looks so putrid, and yet it holds the seeds of new life," Reut said, gazing at the murky water.

"You're talking to a simple guy," I said. "We're not even halfway to where we need to go."

She turned to look at me before saying, "You know as well as I do, happiness doesn't just happen on its own. You have to work at it. It takes time and effort. If a person wants to be happy, he has to know how to change."

"Can we talk about this some night when I'm not so busy?" I asked.

"I'm just wondering," Reut said. "Who's really running away?"

She fell silent, finally returning her gaze to the river and the bank on the other side. Dilapidated wooden houses were scattered among the new apartment blocks and gleaming temples that had sprung up beside the water.

"Sorry," she said. "I'm worried. I'm taking it out on you and that's not fair."

"I understand."

"We were overprotective. So much so that we smothered her. But I didn't think she'd run so far to get away. She doesn't need the money. My father gives her whatever she wants."

"That's exactly what she doesn't want," I said. "She's looking for love, not money. If we can figure out where she found it, we might find out what happened to her."

She gave me a strange look.

"What?" I asked.

"It's my fault."

"Your fault?"

"Yes," she said. "You know, the usual story. Two sisters fall in love with the same man. At least they both think they're in love with him. So they compete for his attention. One wins, and the other is left behind. Except this time the one who got the man was the serious, levelheaded sister, and not the one who really loved him."

"And . . ."

"And it didn't last. It wasn't true love. Sigal hated me for it. That's when it started. She began using. You know how it is. At first, she just wanted to feel better, to forget. Then it became a way to escape from herself. The sad part is that it was my father and I who suggested she go to Thailand to clear her head."

"Clear her head," she repeated bitterly after a pause.

The ferry tied up at the rocking pier of Wat Arun. The monks held their robes close to their bodies, arranged their orange bags on their shoulders, and disembarked quickly, their plastic sandals clicking as they headed toward the temple. We followed behind.

On the pier, a young boy in monk's robes and shaved head was tossing bits of bread to the large catfish in the river. Valium held out his hand and the boy gave him a chunk of bread. Slowly, he rolled the bread between his fingers, letting the crumbs fall into the water. The fish climbed over each other in their eagerness to catch the crumbs in their huge mouths. Reut stood next to him, watching.

"Look how happy they are," Valium said.

"You're not a fish." I laughed. "You can't tell if they're happy."

He turned to look at me. He was standing right beside me, but he was very far away. "You're fucked up, man," he said. "You're not me, so how do you know I can't tell if they're happy?"

I brought my face close to his, so close, in fact, that I could see into the dilated pupils of his eyes. "Yeah, I'm not you. I barely know you. What I do know is that even on your best high, you're not a fish, so I know you can't tell if the fish are happy or not."

"What do you know about what he is or isn't?" Reut challenged me. "You're so sure of your take on the world. It's all so clear to you. Don't you ever question it?"

I considered that for a moment before answering. "Sometimes. For instance, I'm not so sure you're really looking for Sigal. We're not here to find happiness."

"You can be sure," she said. "The only reason I'm in Thailand is to find Sigal. But you're very good at taking me to places where I don't like to go."

Valium was still watching the fish. Then he turned to me again. "Let's start over," he said. "You asked me how I can tell the fish are happy. The question itself assumes that it's possible for them to be happy. When I stand here, I know they are."

Without warning, he turned his back on the water and started walking toward the temple. We followed him. Along the pier was a row of small white stupas, shrines to Buddha. Placed here in this manner, they represented the line between the worldly and the sacred. The temple compound was surrounded by a tall whitewashed wall. The entrance was guarded by two statues of demons with sharp fangs and forbidding eyes holding spears. We walked through the gate into a large courtyard paved in gray bricks. In the center was a big white temple with a red-tiled roof. It was flanked by the wooden structures on stilts that are typical of Thailand. Here they appeared to serve as sleeping quarters for the monks and apprentices.

Young orange-robed monks were sweeping up the fallen leaves of the sacred ficus tree. Chickens wandered the courtyard searching for worms and caterpillars in the moss that grew in the cracks between the bricks. A group of novices was sitting on the steps of a building with pages on their laps. One of them read out the text, beating the rhythm on the step with a small stick. The others repeated after him: "If it is suffering you fear, if it is suffering you abhor, do no evil—overtly or covertly."

We passed a large concrete statue of Buddha. Plain and unadorned, not even painted, it was meant to prevent the students' eyes from growing accustomed to vain beauty. Finally, we reached a big wooden building. A monk was sitting on the worn steps, his head shaved, his orange robe over one shoulder, and his eyes half closed, perhaps basking in the pleasure of the warm sun. Valium stopped beside him and he, too, closed his eyes. We waited. The monk mumbled a mantra, "*Om ah hum vajra siddhi hum.*" His quiet voice was absorbed into the silence around him, reaching beyond images, beyond words.

Valium went inside, with me and Reut on his heels. It was a sleeping hall. Several foreigners were lying on the simple wooden cots. A sour odor hung in the air, the odor of unwashed sheets and clothes that hadn't been changed for days, the characteristic smell of places that offer a cheap bed for the night.

There was a small sink against the wall. An emaciated junkie, his skin the jaundiced color typical of your average long-term heroin addict, was washing his face. Taking a tattered green towel from a nail, he dried himself off. I went over and pointed to the people on the beds. "I'm looking for someone," I said.

He turned to me, holding a hairbrush in his right hand.

"An Israeli woman," I added.

He just stared at me.

"Her name is Sigal."

His murky blue eyes, the whites yellowed from jaundice and drugs, opened wide. Slowly he began brushing his shoulder-length hair. "I don't know names," he said. "What's a name anyway? I can't even remember my own. So I'll get a new one." He laughed and went back to his hair, totally ignoring me.

All of a sudden, I felt very tired. Drained. It takes too much energy to deal with these happiness-seekers. My world is black and white: give and take, hit or get hit. I can't get my mind around all this mindlessness.

"This is goodbye," the crazy junkie said. I got that he was talking about his hair.

"It's all coming off, even the eyebrows. I'm gonna look weird." He smiled. The spaced-out drughead was gone, leaving only an inherently human smile.

I don't understand this world, I thought to myself. I grabbed Reut's hand and pulled her near me.

"What?" she stuttered.

"She looks like her," I said to the junkie still smiling at himself in the mirror.

He glanced at her with an obvious lack of interest. "We all look the same, man," he said. "We're all the same. A worthless shell of flesh."

"Come on," I said to Reut. "We're wasting our time here. We won't get anything out of them." We continued our tour of the temple compound. A monk of Western origins was sitting on the steps of one of the buildings. He was a big man, but somehow, he managed to look refined in his shaved head and orange robes. As we drew close, it was Reut who made the *wai* gesture to him. Smiling, he nodded.

"*Sawadee khrup*," she greeted him. "We're looking for someone."

Her voice held a request, not a demand or a bid for attention. A simple request, the type you can't refuse.

The soft morning light fell on the monk like a cloak. He didn't reply, merely examined her studiously, looking deep into her eyes like an ophthalmologist of the soul.

Finally, he spoke. "That doesn't surprise me. Everyone's looking for something. It's a good start. You can speak Hebrew."

"You speak Hebrew?" I blurted. It was a stupid question, but the surprise was real.

He smiled again. "Yes. You might say that in another place in my life I was Israeli. Kibbutz born and bred. But that was long ago and far away. I'm not even sure that man was me anymore. In any case, it was someone who bore my name, the name my parents gave me, that is. Now I only have the name God gave me."

We let that slide, although we would have liked to hear more. But we weren't here to satisfy our native curiosity about an Israeli who had become a Buddhist monk. And I knew he wouldn't tell us any more.

"We're looking for a young woman by the name of Sigal. We think she was here at the temple," I said. "We don't know when, but it's almost certain she passed through or stayed for a while. I assume you know an Israeli they call Valium? He saw her here." Pointing to Reut, I added, "This is her sister. They look alike."

The monk turned sober, dropping the smile and listening attentively.

"It's very important for us to find her or find out what happened to her," I said. "She's in serious danger."

"I would like to help you, just as I try to help everyone who comes here," he said. He paused for a moment, radiating self-possession and serenity. "But you must understand. For these people, this is the end of the road. They have nothing to go back to. The Western world spit them out. Even Bangkok can be a cruel city for those on the fringes of society. The people who come here have nowhere else to go. They are totally alone. Lost souls. We do not ask them who they are or where they are from. Never. We do not ask about the past. We have no interest in past regrets. Or in thoughts of the future. We want simply to give them a little peace of mind in the present. That is all we have to give. She may have been here and she may not. I cannot say."

"Don't you keep any records?"

"We have no record of those who come. Many pass through the temple."

There was nothing more to say.

"You must realize that some come here to die," he went on. "Most are addicts in the final stages of AIDS. They come when their systems start to fail and no hospital will take them. Where else can they go? When they return their souls to their Maker, we burn the bodies and scatter the ashes in the river."

"Isn't that illegal?" I asked.

He held his hands out in a gesture of resignation. "Here? In a place of total forbearance? What meaning do human laws have?"

"I understand what you're saying," Reut said, "but it's very hard for me to accept."

"I know," said the Israeli monk. "You come here fraught with powerful emotions and you expect us to respond accordingly. To share your anxieties. To put it simply, it doesn't work like that. You must let go, and then perhaps Sigal will emerge from wherever she is."

"I know you're right," Reut answered. She lowered her eyes and stood there in silence. Finally, she said, "But the search is all I have left."

"There is a person who may be able to help you," the monk said. "An Israeli. His name is Reuven Badash. Like every place else, Bangkok is essentially a small world. Reuven knows all the Israelis. The ones who come and the ones who go, and especially the ones who get stuck here. You should talk to him."

The name was like a kick up my ass. Reuven Badash? What the hell was he doing in Bangkok? And how come I didn't know? The past surged up and flooded over me like a sewer that had overflowed. All the crud I had buried came back to haunt me. I was knee-deep in shit again.

The monk got up and walked toward the wooden buildings until he vanished from sight, leaving Reut and I alone. We headed for the river.

"Reuven. That's the name Weiss mentioned last night, isn't it?" I asked.

She nodded. We passed a large statue of Buddha facing the river.

"Do you know him?" she asked.

This time it was me who nodded.

From the light falling on the statue at this hour of the morning, the Buddha seemed to have the hint of a smile on his face. Even his "third eye," the small dot on his forehead, looked like a soft, fleshy mole. He was depicted cross-legged, his right hand in his lap, the palm facing upward, and the fingers of his left hand pointing to the earth and the river, drawing strength from them. It was a delusive strength. It suddenly occurred to me that it was no accident that I was in Bangkok. I still didn't know what Reuven had to do with Sigal's disappearance, but there was no doubt in my mind that he was involved. And I realized I was much more than just some random private investigator who had been hired to find her. Reuven had roped me into the case. He'd fucked with me before and he was doing it again. Why? What did he want from me after all these years?

CHAPTER SIXTEEN

We were on the ferry again, on the way back to the city, leaning on the railing. The water lapped against the side of the boat. Long-tail boats crowded with tourists in loud shirts sounded their horns as they made their way along the river, their noisy motors leaving a white wake behind them. The tourists snapped endless pictures and waved to the passengers of every other tourist boat they passed, who waved back in return. The Bangkok they saw, with its imposing sites and colorful markets, was nothing like the Bangkok we were seeing. Once you cross the thin line to the dark side of the city, it's not so easy to come back. And that's what Sigal had done. I was trying to figure out why.

"Hey there," Reut said with a smile. "You're a million miles away."

If things were different, it might have been a romantic moment. We were standing next to each other, but we weren't really close. At least not as close as I would have liked.

"How do you know Reuven?" she asked.

What could I tell her?

The hyacinths floated past on their way downriver. At some point they would attach themselves to the bank and begin to spread out. One would blossom and another would wither as they fed off each other. And then some would detach themselves from the soil and float on the water until they reached their next foothold. That was the way of the world. What could I say about Reuven? We grew up together. For years we were best friends working side by side for the Security Agency. For years we went out on missions together and saw the unspoken fear oozing from the pores of the other. Out in the field, I always knew that if Reuven was around, someone had my back. And he felt the same about me.

But then Yussuf, our most reliable informant in the Jenin refugee camp, was picked up by the Palestinians. They employed the same methods we do, what we like to call "moderate physical persuasion." They learned a lot from us. Yussuf talked. He didn't just talk, he spilled his guts, and it brought down a whole network it had taken years to build. Someone had screwed up, and it could only have been me or Reuven. It was simple: if Yussuf was blown, one of us was to blame.

These things happen. People make mistakes. But our fuck-up came at the end of March 2002, a few days before the Battle of Jenin. The timing—how should I put it?—wasn't a fluke. In any case, Yussuf broke and blew his cover. Maybe he decided he didn't want to ruin their only chance of getting the upper hand over us. The only thing we knew for sure was that Reuven and I were in charge of the sector, and we were completely in the dark. We had no hint of what was about to happen in Jenin, of what they were setting in motion, of the hundreds of anti-personnel mines and IEDs they were preparing. We had no idea that Jenin was about to be the site of one of the bloodiest battles in history between Israel and the Palestinians.

First, they sent us his head. Then we got his whole hide, after they skinned him, a custom reserved for traitors.

The press was full of the military fiasco. It was so stunning and painful that there was hardly any mention of the botched intelligence.

* * *

It started with an internal inquiry. That was at the stage when they were still trying to cover their asses. It's normal procedure: the system protects itself. The committee took its time before issuing its conclusions, but Reuven and I didn't need time to get the picture. We knew we'd screwed up, or at least one of us had, and we blamed each other. That's how we went from best friends to worst enemies. There was nothing loud or vulgar about our mutual hatred. It was cold and distant. A total break.

But someone had to pay the price.

It wasn't long before we were both out on our asses. And following regulations, they froze our pensions. We were left with only unemployment benefits to get by. There was nothing we could do about it. So we each went our separate ways.

What could I tell her? That my former friend was now a corn under my skin, the kind that leaves a root even after you remove it, and the minute you apply a little pressure it's back? "Reuven is an old wound that never healed," I said finally. "A wound that aches with every change of season or scenery."

"Do you want to tell me what happened?"

"There was a screw-up. We were both involved. We both paid the price. But we never settled accounts between us."

"He blamed you?"

"Yup. He couldn't admit that he made a mistake. After the inquiry, I got up and left. They made it clear to him that it was in his best interest to do the same. He thought I set him up to take the rap. Then he vanished off the face of the earth. I heard rumors that he was training drug runners in Columbia or hunting for diamonds in Angola. I don't know if they're true or not. And now, all of a sudden, he turns up in Bangkok."

Reut put a gentle hand on my arm. "Most of us have something in our past we'd rather not talk about," she said.

"As far as I'm concerned," I answered, "the past is the past."

I was standing with my back to the bank of the river when the boat tied up. That's why I didn't see the change on Reut's face when she looked down at the pier. When I turned around, I saw them. Ivan the Durian with his spiky dog collar and his arms crossed on his chest, and beside him, two strapping local thugs who looked astonishingly like the ones who had beaten me up in the alley. Even if they weren't the same guys, it didn't matter. The principle was the same. Judging by their appearance, given the chance, they'd beat anyone up.

Apparently, Weiss's fuse had gotten shorter since yesterday. Just how short, I didn't know.

"Stay behind me when we get off," I told Reut. Out of the corner of my eye, I saw a stall selling grilled octopus near the exit from the pier. Even from this distance, I couldn't mistake the oddly shaved head of the vendor. It was Tom's driver, Gai. I wondered how he knew to wait for us here. How many people had been tailing us?

"When the fun starts, go to the octopus stall," I instructed.

We were standing by the exit ramp when the ferry stopped at the rocking pier. We had no choice but to get off.

Approaching the fat Russian, I said, "I bet you a hundred bucks you're the first to hit the water."

Instinctively, he took a step back. Realizing his mistake, he held his ground and grinned. "Lucky for you they not understand," he said, pointing to the two thugs holding their ground. "They die laughing."

I gestured discreetly with my head toward Reut. She got my meaning. They made no attempt to stop her.

"Might as well get the party started," I said, aiming a fist at the jaw of the nearest thug. He swayed in surprise, not expecting such a move from a *falang*. I was just beginning to realize how much my hand hurt before the other one jumped me. On my way down, I caught a glimpse of Reut standing next to Gai. That was all I needed.

I picked myself up slowly.

"What do you want?" I asked Ivan. My kidneys ached. I resolved to stop drinking the local whiskey.

"Weiss want to see you."

"You're an asshole, you know that?" I said.

I walked toward the black limousine. The driver opened the door for me like I was some celebrity. Before I got in, I called to Reut. "Wait for me at the hotel. Don't do anything until I get there."

CHAPTER SEVENTEEN

CONTRARY TO ITS name, the Royal Palatine Hotel is a three-star rat trap. The limousine pulled up to the shaded entrance and the doorman showed us in with a bored glassy-eyed expression, the kind that says, "I see nothing, especially nothing I'm not supposed to see." As soon as we entered the run-down lobby, I realized why Weiss had chosen this place to conduct his business. It was way out of the spotlight.

I crammed into the narrow elevator with Ivan and the two thugs. Ivan stank.

"Why don't you do the world a favor and use deodorant," I complained.

We rode up one floor to a corridor with a row of what appeared to be identical offices. On each door was a small sign with the name of a company. They didn't give a lot away. We stopped in front of a sign reading "Weiss Import-Export Inc."

Ivan opened the door. In the hotel's effort to save on electricity, the office was even darker than the corridor, lit only by a few dim lamps.

Alex Weiss was sitting behind a large, highly polished desk facing the door. He was wearing a deep blue military-style suit with epaulets, brass buttons, and short sleeves. His ponderous arms were stretched out motionless on the desk. Several gold chains hung from his broad neck, each of them heavy enough to anchor a boat. They held a collection of weights in the shape of square or triangular amulets with a little Buddha in the center. One also bore a lingam, the penis-shaped amulet that serves as Shiva's phallic symbol. A few bigger lingams sat on the desk, perhaps functioning as paperweights, along with a vase of incense sticks with split heads holding a variety of bills: dollars, rubles, bahts. On the corner of the desk was a yellow-white canary hopping about inside a small straw cage. Tarot cards were spread out in front of it.

Weiss didn't bother to raise his head when we came in. His eyes were pinned on the canary. He opened the cage and it hopped out, pecked at one of the cards, and returned to its cage. He tossed it a few seeds from a bag on the desk, and the bird pecked at them, chirping happily. Still without raising his eyes, Weiss spluttered, "Ivan, you stupid motherfucker, tell the fish sauce to wait outside. I can't stand the smell. You don't smell so good either."

Ivan gestured to the thugs. Obediently, they left the room. When they were gone, Weiss turned over the card the canary had selected, glanced at it briefly, and then placed it back on the desk, facedown.

"Judgment," he said. "Not good. I've been asking questions all day, looking for the answers. The bird picks the cards. And what do they tell me? That everything's an illusion and I don't have the means to find the answers. Me, Weiss, can't find the answers? I'm a serious businessman. You know what the Chinese call me?" Finally, he looked up at me. I shook my head.

"Mr. Ten Percent."

I kept silent.

"You know why? Because they know I take an honest commission off the top of every deal. Not ninety percent and not eleven percent. Ten percent precisely. You get my meaning? But I don't have my ten percent this time. The whole shipment has gone missing. Where is it? That's what I want to know."

He swept the cards onto the floor. I'd already met enough jerks for one day, but I refrained from comment.

Instinctively, Ivan bent down and picked up the cards, examining them closely.

"*Pizdetz*, boss," he said. "Cunts. I look and I see. All cards naked cunts. And all white cunts. Big tits, like in Russia. On Star and World, naked cunts with orange veil like Thailand monks. *Blyad*. I say maybe girl hiding in temple. She put orange veil around her to hide cunt. Maybe also hide money in temple?"

Weiss looked stunned. Finally, he said, "Come here, my little pussycat."

Ivan moved closer. Weiss rose, picked up a large ceramic lingam, and smashed it down on his head. The lingam shattered, but it didn't seem to have any effect on Ivan. He merely scratched the point of impact, like someone scratching their head in embarrassment. I was sure it wasn't the first time it had happened. Weiss sat back down, looking calmer. Ivan spread the cards out on the desk again, facedown as before. The loud noise had sent the canary cringing in a corner, but as soon as Ivan finished arranging the cards, it chirped, hopped out of its cage, and pecked at one.

"Two geniuses," Weiss said. "The bird and the retard."

He eyed me, still considering whether or not to turn the card over. "Is she there? In the temple?"

Again, I shook my head. He didn't move his eyes away until he decided he was satisfied with the answer.

"Like Ivan said the first time he tried to make friends with you, you and me, we're partners, whether you like it or not. That's just how it is. Israelis look out for each other, right?"

"Whatever you say."

He ignored the hostility in my tone.

"You find the girl and we split it down the middle," he went on. "You get the girl and I get the package. Capito?" He didn't wait for my answer. "Girls are like flies around here. Every race, color, and type you can name. You see the Russians? Premium class. Every one of them has a degree. A PhD in physics, an MA in education, it doesn't matter. Here, all of them are studying life sciences."

I didn't respond.

"You want an example?"

Again, he didn't wait for an answer before pressing a small button on his desk.

The most beautiful Russian bombshell I'd ever seen emerged from behind a Chinese screen. Everything about her was absolutely divine. Flowing blond hair, exquisite face, long slender body, amazing boobs.

"Galina, my lovely, what's Einstein's formula for the speed of light?" Weiss asked her.

She didn't blink. "E equals mc squared."

"See? All my whores are educated."

I nodded.

I was still scanning her, my eyes pausing at the interesting bits, each one worth a zoom-in.

"Life isn't easy," Weiss said. "You can see how rewarding my business is, but it also has its irritations. I'm a hard man. I'm used to getting what I want. There aren't many things left that I don't already have. But I'm not going to let some little bitch with no manners and no education play me for a fool. You get it?" His face got redder as his voice rose, but I could see the effort he was making to control his temper. He closed his eyes and took three deep breaths before opening them again.

"Go find the girl and get me my package and my money. Capito?"

"What makes you think I can find her?" I asked.

He was trying very hard not to fly off the handle. He wasn't used to doing things this way. Ordinarily, he'd tell Ivan and his stooges to make mincemeat of me, but instead he closed his eyes again and stretched his arms out on the desk in the position they were in when I first came in. Then he took three more deep breaths and let the air out slowly before opening his eyes. "They say you're a pain in the ass that never leaves empty-handed."

"Assuming I find her, give me one good reason why I should tell you."

That's all it took. He lost it. He was furious, and this time he couldn't control it.

"You think you're a big man, huh? Big enough not to give a shit."

"Boss," Ivan interrupted. "He can't talk to you like that. You want I stomp on him a little?"

"Ivan, my darling, he's like every Israeli. They think they can piss on a tree and the fruit will fall into their hands. He doesn't know us."

"I can teach him some respect, boss," Ivan answered. "He scratched the Mercedes."

I knew exactly what to do to shake the idiot up and take the air out of him. It was my specialty in the agency, psychological warfare. All it takes to pull the rug out from under someone is a few well-aimed provocations they can't handle. It makes them see the fear they keep buried deep down inside. I was very adept at it.

I moved closer to the desk. The canary hopped out of its cage to peck at the seeds scattered about and made the chirping sounds that happy little songbirds make. With a single swift motion, it was in my hand. I turned it over, puffed on its chest to separate the feathers, and pulled out a handful of tail feathers.

The canary shrieked, Ivan the Durian's jaw dropped, and Weiss went white. Literally. All the blood drained from his face. "You know where you can shove these fucking feathers," I said, laying them on top of the cards. I walked out of the room at a measured pace. No one stopped me. Out of the corner of my eye, I saw him pick up the bird and stroke it gently.

CHAPTER EIGHTEEN

ONCE AGAIN, NIGHT fell on the city, bringing with it loneliness and alienation, crime and brutality, cold and emptiness. At night, beliefs are shattered, relationships reveal themselves to be fickle and meaningless, and the city is covered in a heavy blanket of despair.

My next stop was Barbu—Yair Shemesh. We used to be friends.

When Mama Dom mentioned the "angel for all Israel *falang*," I thought she meant Barbu. I knew now that I was wrong. She was referring to Reuven. The cab driver who gave me the amulet from "Buddha of the West" was also talking about Reuven. The pieces were beginning to fall into place. If there was anyone in Bangkok who could clue me in on Reuven, it was Barbu. And he'd know where Reuven was.

What about me? I wondered. Do I know where I am? I still had no idea if I was getting any closer to Sigal, but it was obvious I was getting closer to my past. Maybe they were one and the same.

It wasn't an easy decision for me to go talk to Barbu. There was too much baggage between us, in fact, between the three of us, Reuven, Barbu, and me, a triangle we once believed was eternal. Going there meant asking for a favor, and favors aren't in my vocabulary. I have to admit there was quite a bit of ego involved, but ego also played a practical role: it fostered the fear of opening old wounds, a fear I had carried for years and was still with me here, in Bangkok. It's amazing how people like us are fearless when it comes to operations. But this fear stuck to us like chewing gum, stretching out for miles of time. Still, in the maze I was caught in at the moment, Barbu seemed the only ray of light.

An eponymous purple octopus gleamed in lurid neon lights above the entrance to the club. One of its tentacles was wound around the chest of a cartoon-like girl with fleshy lips, the tip reaching to the space between her legs, which were spread open crudely. I climbed the stairs to the second floor. Ever since the city passed a law banning live shows at street level, Patpong has lost something of the free flesh market atmosphere it once had. The clubs moved the lewder shows upstairs, forcing the tourists to traipse up and down. They go up, take a look, maneuver among all the girls trying to lure them in, and then decide whether to go back down and try the next place, which is exactly the same, or stay there and pay up. You don't get anything unless you pay. There are no free lunches in the world, and certainly not in a Bangkok nightclub.

A skinny man with a pockmarked face came down the stairs toward me. "Where you going?" he asked sharply. A Thai with a pockmarked face can be just as nasty as one with a mole beside his nose, I reminded myself. "To see Barbu," I answered.

I went inside. This early in the evening, the club was still half-empty. I caught sight of Barbu right away. He was sitting at a small table at the end of the bar. Smoke rose from a Gitanes in the ashtray in front of him. The same brand he used to smoke. Strong and aromatic, a lit Gitanes accompanied him wherever he went. Nit Nuy, the Thai woman who had lived with him for years, was behind the bar washing glasses and cleaning ashtrays. Soft music issued from the stereo system. It was jazz from the '50s, his favorite music. A small python was curled up at his feet. From time to time, he reached down and scratched the side of its head.

* * *

Everyone knew him as Barbu. Few remembered, or ever knew, his real name. Even I called him Barbu. It was hard for me at first. For me he was Yair from down the street, Yair from paratrooper training, Yair who always looked so proud in the pictures of him in his uniform with a red beret, paratrooper's wings, and reddish-brown boots. It was only years later, when he was shuttling back and forth between Marseille and Casablanca, that he grew a beard under his Ray-Ban shades and started going by the name Barbu. I guess that was the time when his darker side began to take over. But we only found that out later, when it all collapsed and he simply got up one day, handed in his resignation, and vanished.

Now and then, his name came up in conversation. Presumably, he was in the merchant marine for a while. After that he came back to Israel and started crafting hand-sewn sandals. He lived in one of the old stone houses on the Haifa shore, where his friends would come to listen to jazz and puff hesitantly on a joint, grinning from ear to ear. Yair never smoked weed. He just sat there and smiled, rocking his head in time to the music and scratching his mangy German shepherd behind the ear. Its name was Jazz, naturally.

One day he closed up shop and disappeared. There were rumors. They said he moved to Amsterdam and after that to New York. He was seen at the Bhagwan ashram in Pune in India. Then nothing for years. Until I ran into him one day in Bangkok.

I was walking through Patpong looking for a quiet place to have a drink. The Goldfinger was too loud and the French Kiss was too crowded, filled, as usual, with journalists and mercenaries waiting for a war to keep them busy and meanwhile consuming huge quantities of beer until their bloated bellies were leaning on the bar. So I went into the Purple Octopus, hoping that it would be quiet upstairs. I was right. That's when I saw Yair.

I went over to him. He didn't even get up, just kept sipping on a frosted glass of Coke and ice. "Just so you know," he said, "here I'm Barbu. And that's Nit Nuy," he added, pointing to an attractive petite woman behind the bar.

I sat down and drank the whiskey Nit Nuy poured me. We exchanged a few words, like two people who hadn't seen each other in a long time but weren't really interested in the usual meaningless Israeli protocol of "where have you been and what have you been doing?" In any case, it made no difference where we were in our lives at the moment. "What's up?" I asked him, as if we'd seen each other the day before.

"Everything's coming up roses," he answered in kind, smiling.

That put us on the same page.

"The whiskey's authentic. No knockoffs here," he said.

"Good to know."

Nit Nuy refilled our glasses, whiskey in mine and Coke and ice cubes in his.

"If you're looking to get laid, let me know, and I'll say *yes* or *no* and *who*," Barbu said. "You don't stick your cock in any of my girls without my say-so. Got it?"

That was Barbu speaking, spelling out the house rules. Not the Yair I knew.

Contrary to my first impression, he was kind and generous. I slept better that night than I had in a long time. Maybe it was the whiskey, or maybe the two girls with the amazingly soft skin I found in my bed in the middle of the night. I didn't even know how they got there, and I didn't really want to know. What difference did it make? They were there. Surprisingly, I fucked that night without any inhibitions or any anxiety about doing something I hadn't done in months. No regard for the future either. Nothing. I just went with the flow. I was harder than I'd been in quite a while, ever since the incident that brought us all down, and afterwards the girls and I cuddled up in the bed, our arms and legs intertwined like a big purple octopus, and I slept like a baby.

The next morning was even better. One of the best of my life, the kind that falls into your lap like a gift. There aren't too many like that. Not for me anyway. I chose to forget the profession of the girls who woke up with me and simply see them as giggly little things with an enormous desire to smother me with attention. So what? We had breakfast on the floor. They fed me the best bits from the bowl with chopsticks and poured me endless cups of green tea. Then we went back to the bed and fucked some more. When I woke up, the bowls were gone and they were sitting against the wall, gazing at me.

"You have Thai girlfriend?" Gong asked. She looked like her name, which means "shrimp"—small, curled over, and not very pretty. I answered in the negative. Her friend, Na-Nao, "cool season," didn't speak any English. She asked Gong what I'd said, and they exchanged a few sentences and giggled.

Na-Nao was tall and dark, suggesting southern, maybe even Muslim, origins. She was much taller than most Thai women and extraordinarily lovely. "Na-Nao say first time she do it with *falang*," Gong reported.

* * *

Once again, I was sitting across from Barbu. Yair Shemesh was gone. He was counting 100-baht notes, leaning over until his beard, already showing flecks of white, was resting on his chest. From time to time, Nit Nuy refilled his glass of Coke and added more ice. No one was allowed to bother him until he was finished counting and had put rubber bands around the wad of bills. Not even an old friend. Not that I was sure I fit that description.

After handing the bills to Nit Nuy, Barbu dragged the snake closer to him by the tail and started scratching it. The python didn't seem to derive any pleasure from the attention, but it was probably used to it.

"So tell me what you're doing here. What is it this time?" Barbu was never one to beat around the bush.

"I'm looking for someone."

"An Israeli?"

"Yes, a young Israeli woman."

Stroking his beard, he said, "I heard a different story."

I didn't reply.

He continued to stroke his beard in a slow rhythmic motion, gazing at me with his black eyes under thick brows. "I heard you wasted a guy, the Israeli gay."

"Bullshit. Why would I want to take him out?"

"Because he wouldn't tell you where they hid the package they stole, him and Sigal."

I ran that through my head. "I don't know what the hell you're talking about," I said.

Barbu gave me a look that said he wasn't in the mood to waste time. "I heard you're working for someone who's looking for a way to make a deal and get her sister and the money out of Thailand."

I laughed. "Doesn't that sound like a fairy tale to you?"

He didn't join in my laughter. "Anything's possible in Thailand," he said. "Two types of people come here. Some are naïve tourists and the others aren't. You certainly don't fall into the first category. You come here for a reason."

"Why would I kill him?" I asked.

"What I want to know," he went on, "is how come you land in Bangkok and a few hours later you happen to take a cab and the driver happens to have two Israeli passports and they happen to belong to two morons who got mixed up in a drug deal. One of them disappeared and the other was killed, and you just happen to be the last person to see him."

"I guess it's all coincidence," I said. It didn't sit well with me, pretending to be an idiot.

"Coincidence my ass," he said, angrily. He grabbed the snake and hurled it at me. I don't know who was more surprised, me or the snake, but there's no doubt about which of us reacted faster. The snake wrapped itself around my leg and sank its teeth into my shin. It hurt like hell, but I kept quiet.

"There's no such thing as coincidence. Don't you know that?" he said. "Everything is part of a predetermined plan."

Whoever said pythons don't bite? When I got it off me, Barbu laughed. "He's an orphan," he said. "He used to belong to an old junkie who performed with him onstage and let him sleep in her cunt. But she died. Of AIDS. Poor little baby. I adopted him. What else could I do? If I hadn't, he would have ended up as soup for some fucking Chinese."

I considered the subject of AIDS and the blood that was dripping down my leg under my pants. I wanted to crush the creature's head, but it had already slithered into a corner and curled up.

"Are you going to help me?" I asked.

He didn't answer.

"You owe me."

"I don't owe anyone anything," he said. "Not you, that's for sure."

"What are you talking about?" I asked.

"Don't you get it yet? You too dumb to understand?" he said.

It's not that I didn't understand. But I wasn't sure I was ready for it.

"Officially, they blamed you. The brass came down hard on you and Reuven when the Jenin network collapsed. So why do you think I had to leave?"

I kept silent. What could I say? Barbu was gone and Yair Shemesh was back, returning me to the past, to the baggage we all still carried.

"You fucked up and I was just collateral damage," he said. "The handler in the field."

Nit Nuy topped up my whiskey glass. I could already feel the headache I was going to have later.

"I left because of you, because I didn't want to take sides. And I didn't want to be there when you started to hate each other."

I was even more silent, if that's possible.

"You didn't know what was happening in the field. You thought everyone was in your debt. Why? Because of the money they got from you every month? You were clueless. Yussuf tried to get a message to us, to tell us he was torn up inside. That things weren't black and white. That it's more complicated, and we're all just pawns in a game. But you couldn't see three feet ahead of you. Nothing. It took Reuven time, but in the end, he got it. That's why he's here. You come and go, blame the whole world, blame him. For you, the penny never dropped."

I didn't respond, letting time and the whiskey do their job.

"I need your help," I said finally.

"I can't help you. The only thing that can help you is letting go of the past. All I can do is give you Reuven's address. After that, you're on your own. And don't come back. It's over between us."

CHAPTER NINETEEN

I WENT BACK out into the humid streets of Bangkok. It was a long time since someone had told me to get lost. I should have been angry, but I wasn't. That told me that Yair Shemesh was fogging my head like a film I had to clean out. But what had just happened? There's no such thing as coincidence, he said. Was he making a general statement or was he hinting, in his own enigmatic way, at what my next move should be?

I replayed in my mind everything that had happened since Shai got the telephone call. The passport the cabbie handed me on a silver platter; the fact that he led me by the nose to Micha Waxman; Reuven. One thing I still didn't understand: Why had I been dragged into this story? Why me, in particular?

I found myself walking through the crowded aisles of MBK, one of Bangkok's largest and busiest shopping malls. I wandered among the mountains of jewelry, knockoff watches, and DVD covers. Pick one, and within ten minutes you'll have a copy. And then coming toward me I saw the laughing eyes of Aliza, Shmulik's secretary from the embassy. It's weird, running into people you know when you're overseas. It doesn't seem plausible.

She was standing in front of me, her arms akimbo, her belly button showing above her tight low-riding jeans. She was wearing an open blouse over a tank top studded with black sequins. However dainty and petite she looked, she still gave the impression of being a very tough gal.

When I got closer, she smiled, her thin lips opening wide to reveal small, sharp teeth like a lizard. "You forgot all about me," she said, in a tone that implied "you're wasting time."

"Hi," I said.

"It's a shame. I can help you. You have no idea how much I can help."

I knew she was right. Wherever you go, the secretary is your key asset. Smile at her, pay her a little attention, and you're riding high.

"You're a big tall guy," she said. "Taller than I remembered."

"Sorry. I'll try to be taller in your memory next time."

"You're stuck, right?" she asked.

Apparently, the look in my eyes said it all.

"Coffee?" I suggested.

* * *

We went into a Starbucks and sat down at a table in the smoking section. Things moved fast. By the time I asked her who Weiss worked for, her fingers were already resting on my hand. No ring and no tan line to indicate that one had ever been there.

I couldn't ignore her scent. She used a Victoria's Secret cream with a fruity perfume. I know, because I used to get it for Mira when I went to New York. That was when I was still trying. I can't say it didn't do anything for me. She closed her eyes. When she opened them, again the smile was gone.

"Mainly the Chinese," she said. "Without them, nothing moves. They control the drug trade. The Israelis just handle the trafficking, and only to Europe. It's frustrating for them."

"Why?"

"Too little profit for too much hassle. You know what Israelis are like, they want it all. God gave them two faults: big eyes and no self-control. Put that together with two other features, no tact and no understanding of other people and places, and you've got a ticking time bomb. They always want more. They show up here flaunting suitcases filled with money and think it's like buying a stall in the market. Eventually they learn they're not playing on their own turf."

She took a pack of Eve Menthols from her purse, lit one, and inhaled deeply.

"Is Weiss in charge of moving the drugs?" I asked.

Again, she closed her eyes, opened them, and exhaled, twisting her lower lip to blow the smoke toward the ceiling.

"You don't think he does it himself, do you? It's a well-oiled machine. He has his errand boys. You already met one of them."

"Shaya?"

"Uh-huh." She nodded.

I waited for her to go on. She rested the cigarette in the ashtray, took a sip of coffee, and cleaned the foam from her lips with the tip of a finger. Her fingers were long and thin, almost as if they had no joints. Just long pale extensions of her hand.

"Everyone knows kids are looking for drugs. So Shaya and the rest of Weiss's agents set up shop in a guesthouse or a bar on Khao San where they roll joints and share them out liberally, all the while bragging about the package they smuggled into Europe. I guess the fish are always dumber than the fisherman."

That made me laugh.

"What are you laughing for?" she asked.

"For some reason, aphorisms about fish are very popular in Thailand."

"I was trying to make a philosophical point, but I guess you know everything," she said resentfully. She wanted to show me there was more to her than I imagined.

"No, I don't know everything. Sometimes I just make a guess, and I don't always get it right."

"What's your guess about me?"

She puffed on the cigarette, revealing her small, sharp teeth. Her eyes were even darker and cloudier than before, making them colder.

"You know more about Weiss than your average embassy worker. You had some connection with him, or you still do," I said.

"Too many fingers started pointing to the embassy," she said cryptically.

We sat in silence, sipping our coffee. Then she went on.

"Had, in the past tense. It's over. Remember that. But I can't change it now. They'll find out when they find out. It won't be the first time the dirty laundry of a Foreign Office worker is aired in public."

"Are you trying to use me to wash it clean?"

"Maybe," she said. "When people come here, they're naïve kids, still wet behind the ears. Every smile seems to open the door to an unknown world. But some are illusions."

I didn't say anything. I knew her world. It was paved with people who had gone down the wrong path.

"I met him at his club," she said. "He was the most un-Israeli Israeli I'd ever known. The ones I'd met before were all like you, sarcastic, damaged. He was charming. A real gentleman. He showed me there were other options."

"And it didn't bother you, how he made his living?"

"I ignored it, or repressed it. Same thing. I didn't talk about the embassy, and he didn't talk about his business. He preferred to talk about Buddhism and mysticism. It was easy for me to forget about work and just have fun."

"How did he get to be so powerful?" I asked.

She puffed on her cigarette before answering. "Weiss always uses the same game plan," she said finally. "He smiles at the backpackers and plays hardball with the Thai. That's what makes him such a good go-between. He knows how much Israelis love to take risks. He can always find someone who shows up here after a year in India. 'I'll make one trip,' they think. 'What can happen. Then I'll take the money and go back to India for another year or two. I'll be able to chill out, drinking chai and puffing on bongs all day.' Weiss and his Thai associates know some of the shipments won't make it through. They factor that in."

"Sounds great in theory. There's just one problem," I said.

"What's that?"

"Micha Waxman didn't just arrive here from India. He lived in Bangkok, high as a kite most of the time, and knew all the suppliers that could help feed his habit. And I have no doubt that he paid in sexual favors. He doesn't fit your description. Neither does Sigal Bardon. Her family is rich. A few months ago, she decides to tour the East and winds up in Thailand. You'd expect her to go to the islands, lie on the beach all day and cut loose at acid parties at night, doing her head in and fucking like a rabbit. But instead, she gets involved in a drug deal and disappears. I still don't know where or how

she met Micha, how they were connected, or whose idea it was
to cash in on the drugs or the money."

While I was talking, Aliza stubbed out her first cigarette
and lit a second. Again, she blew the smoke toward the ceiling
with a twist of her lower lip. And again, she closed her eyes. It
was a tic I already recognized. Opening her eyes, she gave me
an inquisitive look.

"We thought you knew," she said.

I almost missed it. *We?* I wondered who she meant, but I
didn't ask. I removed her hand from mine. Was she working
me? If she was, who was her puppet master? Weiss? Reuven?
One thing I was sure of: she knew what happened to Sigal.

There are no chance encounters. I'd almost fallen into the
trap, *almost* being the operative word. You always have to remember there are only two things that make the world go
round—money and sex. Whether each on its own or both
together.

She opened her mouth as if she was about to say something.
Her sharp teeth gleamed like delicate Chinese porcelain.

"I don't," I said.

Again, she covered my hand with her long, cool fingers.

"I can't say any more. Not now," she said. "Go talk to
Malachi."

"Who's he?"

"An Israeli doing time."

"His name doesn't appear on the list of Israeli prisoners. I've
seen it."

She leaned back in her chair, nearly rocking it, giving herself time to answer.

"He comes from a well-known family. They kept it out of
the media. Don't want anyone to know their son got himself

in trouble. He's in for a long time. Drugs. Not likely to get a pardon. He's in touch with all the *falangs* in the drug trade in Bangkok."

"From prison?" I asked.

She laughed.

I left her sitting there, engulfed in the cloud of smoke rising from the long, thin cigarette between her lips. I signaled goodbye and she waved back, immobile save for the slight movement of her hand. I had no way of knowing that a moment later she would take out her cellphone, press a number, and say, "He's on his way to Malachi."

*　*　*

You never tell a woman about meeting another woman. So I called Reut, told her what had happened with Weiss, and didn't mention my encounter with Aliza.

"I'm going to see an Israeli in prison," I said. "My source says he knows everything that goes on in Bangkok."

I listened to her silence. Finally, she said, "I'm starting to believe we won't find her."

This time it was me who remained silent.

"You know, like a sister's intuition."

"I'll call you when I get back," I assured her. "Can we meet?"

"Yes. I'll wait for you here."

CHAPTER TWENTY

I WENT BACK to the Chao Phraya and got on a large ferry for Nonthaburi on the other side. It was noontime, as hot and humid as only Bangkok can be. The river was as flat and shiny as a mirror, its stillness broken only by the foamy wake behind the ferry. A light breeze momentarily sent a small ripple through the water. The hyacinths bobbed up and down; a long-tail boat sailed by. It took about an hour to reach the last stop. Toward the end of the journey, there were very few passengers left on the ferry. I went up to the top deck and stood next to a young guy who pulled off the rubber band holding his long blond hair in a pony tail to let his curls fly about in the breeze.

"Bangkok Hilton?" he asked with a smile.

I nodded. It was only logical to assume that everyone still on the boat was heading for the same place, the Bang Kwang men's prison, known as the Bangkok Hilton by the foreigners incarcerated there.

"Going to visit a prisoner?" the guy asked.

"Yes, an Israeli by the name of Malachi Razon. It means 'skinny angel' in Hebrew."

"Heroin?"

I nodded again. Most of the foreigners in Thailand's "correctional institutions" are doing time for smuggling heroin into Europe or Africa. Now and then you get a pedophile or a murderer.

"What about you?" I asked.

"It's trendy in Khao San these days to visit a prisoner. I guess beaches and acid parties don't do it for us anymore. I'm curious to see if what they show in movies like *Bangkok Hilton* is true. I went to see a Brit yesterday. Today I'm going to visit someone else."

"How was it?"

"Depressing. I didn't get to ask him a single question about life in prison. He didn't stop talking about how he was going to use the power of his mind to teleport himself outside the walls. If it wasn't that, it was the insect noises the prisoners make. I was there for an hour and a half and he didn't shut up for a second. He wore me out."

"But you're still going back?"

"I feel it's the least I can do for someone confined to the world's asshole," he said. "You know how it is, the thought that 'there but for the grace of God go I.'"

We arrived at the last ferry stop and everyone disembarked. First off was an elderly couple carrying a heavy straw basket, he in shorts and flip-flops and she in a flowery dress. They were followed by a young couple in tight black clothes and gold chains. My long-haired friend and I brought up the rear.

We passed the market selling vegetables and fish and turned left at the first corner. That's where the famous Thai smile vanishes. In front of us was the tall gray prison wall. In the courtyard outside is the visitor screening post under a sign reading "Bang Kwang Central Prison." Just so you know where you are.

If you want to get in before noon, you have to arrive at the gate by ten thirty and fill out a form. It asks for the visitor's name, passport number, and nationality, and the prisoner's name and block number.

I filled in the details—Malachi Razon, Block 3—and handed it to a guard with a pockmarked face whose attention was focused on a bowl of soup that smelled of fish oil. He worked his chopsticks deftly, dripping soup on the form, but he didn't seem to care. Just as he couldn't care less about some *falang* rotting inside. He glanced at what I had written, waiting to finish his soup before doing anything else. When he was done, he lit a cigarette under a "no smoking" sign, asked for the pen in the pocket of my shirt, scribbled a signature, took the carton of phony Marlboros I had bought in Patpong the night before for ten dollars, and gave me back the signed form. We walked to the visitor area, the whole group from the ferry making our way together. From the other side of a chain fence, a row of prisoners was led in. The first two were Thai and the other two foreigners, one black and one white, the latter presumably Malachi. I've seen a lot of ghastly sights in my time, but this is one I never get used to: leg shackles making their macabre noise and symbolizing more than anything else the drastic change in a person's life. Kids who used to be carefree backpackers were now convicts in one of the worst prisons in the world. The black guy's face broke into a broad grin, and my ferry companion parted from me with a wave of his hand as he walked toward him. Malachi didn't smile.

The shackles were old and rusty and dug into the flesh. The wounds had healed around them, making them an integral part of his body. He sat down across the table from me, coughed a few times, wiped the phlegm away with his hand, and asked, "Why did you come on Friday?"

I wasn't sure I'd heard him right, but when it sunk in, I was stunned. When was the last time anyone came to see the asshole? He lived like a rat surrounded by starving cockroaches, and the timing of my visit didn't suit him?

"I keep Shabbat," he said, coughing heavily. His dull eyes flitted back and forth to the guards sitting in the corner. As far as he was concerned, I could get up and leave. He didn't give a damn that I'd come.

"Okay, but I'm already here and I don't know when I'll be able to come back," I said.

"After sundown tomorrow."

His face was scrawny. Several of his teeth were chipped and others were black. Drugs do that to you; they rot the teeth. There were cuts on his cheek and ear that didn't look good. I guessed that someone had hit him with a brick, and the wounds were festering. That could do him in.

A rat ran across the floor. Neither the prisoners nor the visitors gave it a second glance. The guards didn't pay it any mind either.

"You look sick," I said.

He laughed. "Sick? I was already on my way to the morgue, but what I saw in the hospital convinced me to get out of there fast."

I remained silent. Letting him vent was a good start. He played with the sidelocks hanging down from his typical prison haircut, a shaved head. He undoubtedly had to pay a heavy price for those limp curls.

"What was wrong with you?" I asked offering him a cigarette from the pack of Marlboros I'd brought with me. It's common practice to bring prisoners cigarettes. They're the coin of the realm behind bars. Sometimes a pack is used to transfer cash, with a few of the smokes replaced by tightly rolled-up bills. The guards know all about it. They take their fifty percent cut during the body search when the inmate leaves the visitor area.

I saw the hesitation on his face. "It's Shabbat, and I quit smoking anyway." But his eyes kept going back to the pack I left on the dirty wooden shelf under the double wire partition between us. "Food poisoning. Didn't stop shitting, like it was shooting out of every hole. I thought I was gonna die. I prayed to God to get it over with fast. I was so weak I couldn't stand up. In the end, they sent me to the hospital. It looked like something out of the Middle Ages during the plague. Ninety-nine-point-nine percent mortality rate."

The rat made its way across the room, keeping close to the wall where the prisoners were sitting. I noticed one of the Thai prisoners give it a hungry look. The protein on the menu was getting away. "We sleep on the floor, shoulder to shoulder, toe to toe. It's no wonder disease spreads quickly. The last thing they want is an epidemic in the prison. It's bad for business."

"But you recovered," I said. Not that he looked healthy, but at least he didn't seem to be at death's door.

He laughed, again revealing his rotting teeth. "Praise God. I made it out of there. Somehow, they cured me. It was a miracle." He coughed, and then went on with his story. "The first day in the hospital, I fell out of bed. And the beds are high. Forget the diarrhea, it's lucky I didn't break my neck. I forgot how to sleep in a bed. All around me were locals dying of AIDS or one of the other curses that get you when your immune system is gone. I just wanted to get out of there. And their screams. You never heard anything like it. The guards shoot junk into them to make them scream. They tell them it's a cocktail to cure AIDS. I guess when your immune system isn't working, it hurts even more. I kept praying like some religious fanatic. Lord have mercy on me. When the doctor came by in the morning, he asked if I had any money. I said yes. He got the money, and by the afternoon I got the medicine. It helped."

We both sat in silence for a moment, and then he said, "You wouldn't wish this life on your worst enemy. The best you can hope for here is a fair trial and an easy hanging. I'd do anything to get out of here. God willing, I will."

"What are you in for?"

He laughed again. "Same as everyone. They picked me up at the airport trying to smuggle drugs to Amsterdam. Just another nitwit who thought it wouldn't happen to him. They looked at my passport and saw I flew back and forth from Bangkok to Amsterdam. Sometimes Bombay or Goa. You don't have to be a genius to put two and two together. They caught me with a K and a half of heroin."

I could see the beautiful beaches of Goa in my head, the chance meeting on a moonlit night followed by the request to take a small package with you on the flight to or from Bangkok. They're always sure they won't get caught.

But Malachi was different. He was no naïve jerk. And his faith made him even tougher. I wondered how long he'd been doing it and who was putting money in his prison account.

You can't survive in the Bangkok Hilton without money. They don't take plastic here, just cash. You draw it out little by little, only as much as you need each time. It's too dangerous to have a thousand-baht bill in your hand. You're likely to get slaughtered like a rat for lunch.

"I can help you," I said.

He started to laugh and then swallowed it. "You? Who do you think you are? The only ones who can help me are God and the king of Thailand. In that order. The first one is with me all the time. The second, I have to wait for his next birthday and maybe I'll get a pardon."

"All that tells me is that your friends, including Alex Weiss, are happy to let you rot here," I said.

He gave me a dirty look, coughed, and spit the phlegm out on the floor. "You come here, I don't know who the hell you are, and you try to fuck with my head."

"Trust me," I said, taking a stab in the dark, "I know what I'm talking about. I've seen too many Israelis in your situation. For the first year, your friends come to visit. Then they scatter to the four winds. They each have their own story. One is being investigated in France, another is extradited to Columbia. All that's left is your family. Do you want them to see you like this? A year ago, you were a young man with his whole life ahead of him. Next year you'll be an old man with nothing to look forward to."

My words ignited a tiny spark in his eye. For a man serving life in prison, *maybe* is the last glimmer of hope: *maybe* they'll transfer him to Israel, *maybe* the king will grant him a pardon on his next major birthday. I did the math. If he'd been in Thailand for a while, he probably had a local girlfriend. They always do. And since she wanted her *falang* to take her with him when he went back to the good life in Europe, she must have made sure to have his child as soon as possible.

"Did she have your kid circumcised?" I asked.

"That's what keeps me awake at night," he answered.

Bingo. "Does she visit you?"

"No. In the beginning she used to come once or twice a month. The first year, they even let us have conjugal visits. After we fucked, she'd complain she didn't have enough money. You know what they're like. As soon as you stop giving them money, they forget about you. All I know is that she sent the kid to live with her parents in the country and she went back to the bar where I met her, in Nana Plaza. I don't give a damn about her anymore, but it's killing me to think that my baby is being brought up to herd buffalo in some village in northern Thailand instead of getting a proper Jewish education."

"I can arrange for him to be adopted in Israel," I said, stretching the truth. I had no idea if that was at all possible by Thai law, but I left it for later to find out. My job now was to manipulate his emotional state—Tactic no. 5 in the Security Agency handbook.

He didn't respond. But he was nobody's fool. "Assuming you can, what do you want in exchange?" he asked finally.

"Sigal Bardon," I said. "If she's still alive."

Again, he coughed and spit on the floor. "How do I know you'll keep your part of the bargain?"

"You have my word," I said. "Nothing else matters. You know that."

"Give me a cigarette."

I passed him a cigarette and a lighter. The guard didn't react. I knew he'd extract payment from Malachi later. Malachi lit the cigarette and inhaled deeply. "That's so good," he said. "Look, all the big shots in the drug trade are looking for her. Half the officers in the Bangkok police, the Chinese, Weiss— they're all looking for her."

Check, I thought. Sigal's alive. Score one for me.

He took another drag on the cigarette, coughed again, and spit again. "It's not just the 21K of heroin and the money. She flipped them off. They all have to depend on their mules. Without them, they wouldn't be where they are. They can't allow them to turn the tables on them. One mule changing the rules? They can't tolerate that. Can you imagine what it does to their image? The shipment disappeared and Sigal disappeared with it. They'll find her. Trust me. They found Micha Waxman, didn't they? And they took him out. When they find Sigal, she'll be gone for good."

"Do you know where she is?" I asked.

That made him laugh, and the laughter made him cough until he was almost choking. "You're killing me," he said, coughing up more phlegm and spitting it out. "If I know, that means *they* know, and as far as you're concerned, it's already too late."

He took a final drag on the cigarette and crushed it out regretfully. The guard stood up and said something in Thai.

"I have to go," Malachi said.

"One last question. Who set Sigal up with Weiss?"

He gave me a hard look. "I thought you knew," he said. "I thought he was a friend of yours."

"Who?" I asked, shocked by his answer. "Reuven?"

He nodded, stood up, and began walking away, dragging with him the shackles and their horrific noise.

* * *

I was standing outside the Bangkok Hilton. The river in front of me didn't offer any comfort. I felt as if someone had brought a five-ton hammer down on my head. It's impossible, I thought. Sigal Bardon and Reuven? How could that be?

CHAPTER TWENTY-ONE

LIFE IS FULL of surprises. Some are so mind-blowing you don't think they're possible. Things like that only happen in movies. Certain types of movies, that is. By the time I left Bang Kwang Prison, it was already late afternoon. The trip back to Banglamphu took about an hour. From there I took a motorbike taxi to the corner of Silom and Patpong. Whenever I hire the services of one of the drivers waiting for fares in their bright blue or orange jackets, I feel like I'm taking my life in my hands. I also get an adrenaline rush. The former comes from knowing that most of them are addicted to ya-ba amphetamines, and the latter from speeding among the smoking buses and tuk-tuks moving laboriously through the heavy traffic. Along the way, your trousers brush up against the barely moving vehicles, and you may very well fold back the side mirror on a cab, but you keep racing forward.

Late afternoon is a strange time. The hot, humid morning and midday hours drain all life and sensuality out of you. But as the day goes by and the sunlight becomes more muted, people are lured out of their cooler holes and the city opens like a flower.

* * *

I headed for Patpong 3, the street where Micha Waxman had been killed. I'm not quite sure what brought me there. Maybe I hoped that if I went back to the scene of the crime, I'd find something I missed the first time.

Sitting in one of the bars flanking the narrow street, you can see everyone sauntering by, and everyone sauntering by can see you observing them. Everybody's eyeing and being eyed, watching and being watched. There's nowhere to hide. I found Shmulik, the embassy security chief, in the bar adjacent to the site of Micha Waxman's murder.

Bingo number two.

I took the stool next to him. For a while, he just looked at me without talking. Eventually he said, "Want a drink?"

"Beer," I answered.

He gestured for the barman, who came over with a broad grin on his face.

"Glass?" he asked.

I shook my head. Don't drink from a glass in Bangkok. You never know what's lurking on the rim: herpes, gonorrhea, or just undefined gunk. A minute later, a cold bottle of beer in a felt sleeve was sitting in front of me.

"The embassy knows," Shmulik said. "I never kept it a secret."

"I didn't know," I said. "You managed to surprise me. When did you come out?"

"When I started traveling the world. That's why I took a job with the Foreign Office. I knew it meant I'd be in places like this, places like Bangkok, where no one cares about your sexual orientation."

"Not even if you're a security officer?"

"As long as you pass your annual polygraph, who cares?"

"Who cares?" I repeated, my voice rising a little. "You've been here a while so you must have known Micha Waxman."

His response was immediate. The blood drained from his face.

"I knew him," he whispered. "He was such a pretty boy when I met him. Sweet. All heart."

"And you didn't know anything about him? You? The embassy's chief security officer?"

Shmulik exploded. "How was I supposed to know he'd start selling his body? How was I supposed to know he'd get hooked on heroin?"

"Are you delusional?" I was well aware of the contempt and loathing in my voice.

"I let you down, huh? You can't deal with the fact that there are gays in the agency. You'd be happier if I turned out to be a maniac and you didn't have to find out that one of your former agency colleagues was gay."

"You talk too much. How did you meet him?" I asked

"A friend of a friend had a garden party at the Hilton," he said with a laugh. "All the Israelis living in Bangkok were invited. I exchanged small talk with a few people, had a drink or two. Didn't find anyone I really wanted to talk to. I was fed up with the usual conversations. You know what it's like when Israelis get together overseas. All they do is gossip. I wandered outside. The hotel has a beautiful tropical garden, palm trees, elephant ears. The best part was that the whole garden was suffused with the scent of honeysuckle. To this day, I remember the perfume. It was like I had to cut through it as I walked, it was that thick. At the end of the garden, on the bank of a canal, is one of the strangest shrines in Bangkok. A mass of lingams, phalluses, symbolizing the Hindu god Shiva. It's an impressive collection, every possible size, shape, and material. Micha was there, sitting on a bench. Handsome, well built, surrounded by erect penises and enveloped in the most intoxicating scent you can imagine. He was magnificent, not the scared strung-out junkie you knew."

Shmulik fell silent. His rugged face looked softer and his boxer hands rested lightly on the table. He picked up his bottle and guzzled down the beer, as if talking, or his memories, had dried him out. Then he went on. "I wanted to fuck him right there. And I would have, if two stupid girls hadn't shown up and started giggling at the penises. Dumb blonds who don't have time for anything except themselves and the fake Gucci bags in the stalls. I detested them for ruining the moment. I didn't dare approach him after that. All I had left was the scent. Then one day I ran into him again in one of the bars around here."

I remembered the odor that hung in the air over Micha's body. I never knew murder could smell like honeysuckle. Was it Shmulik? The boy said he saw a fat, bald foreigner.

"He could see I was salivating with lust," Shmulik said resentfully, "and it made him laugh. I hated that laugh. We got together every night after work for two months."

"Where?"

"Here, or someplace else. Bangkok is full of places only the gays know about. We'd have a drink and then go to one of the love hotels and fuck."

"When did you find out he was a junkie?"

"When he started asking for money. In the beginning, I thought he was in love with me. After a while I understood that all I was for him was an ATM. He was no different from all the other whores in Thailand."

"When was the last time you saw him?"

"About a week ago. He was going on about being able to get his hands on a large sum of money. He wanted a sex change operation. He said he gave me love and I didn't give him anything in return. If I didn't help him, he'd have to do something terrible." He looked down. "But I didn't pay it any mind. He was always moody."

"What did he mean, *something terrible*?" I asked.

"I have no idea. Who cares," Shmulik said.

I put three hundred-baht notes on the counter and got up.

"What are you going to do?" I asked.

"Don't know." I could hear the sadness in his voice.

* * *

I walked away down the street, not turning to look back. I don't think I wanted to hear any more. Not then, at least. I just wanted to get as far away as possible, away from the filth all around me. I didn't want to know who killed Micha Waxman, and I wasn't even sure anymore that I wanted to know where Sigal was hiding and why she had run. It all seemed too dark, like I was swimming in a huge cesspool. All I wanted was to breathe fresh air.

CHAPTER TWENTY-TWO

THE EARLY EVENING is the best time of day to sit beside the pool at the Oriental. Elliptical Chinese lanterns sway from the branches of the coconut palms, casting a red glow on the still water. On the horizon, you can see the sun setting quickly over the Chao Phraya, lighting the sky in its vivid colors. The hotel workers start collecting the empty cocktail glasses and removing the mattresses from the deck chairs.

She was stretched out on a chaise, long and serene. Her straw hat was on the deck beside her, along with an open book on the life of Buddha. I glanced at the title of the chapter, "Mission and Death." She looked every inch a tourist without a care in the world.

"To your credit, you look very relaxed," I said.

She laughed. It sounded like marbles rolling down a hill, gently tapping against each other. This is the first time I've heard her laugh, I thought.

"Would it help if I looked upset?" she asked.

"No. It wouldn't change things one little bit."

I was dying to pass my fingers over her smooth skin. Everything about her stimulated the nerve endings in my body. Her thighs were the most sensuous things I'd ever seen.

I imagined myself kissing her fingers, one by one. Her round shoulders looked absolutely perfect with her long hair curling gently over them.

"You're devouring me with your eyes," she said, looking me straight in the eye as no other woman ever had.

"You're right," I said. "I don't know what's come over me."

She laughed again and I envisioned myself picking her up in my arms and carrying her back to her room, kicking the door closed like the hero of some romance novel before falling onto the bed with her. After everything I'd seen in the past few days, I was hungry for her, for human warmth and sensibilities. But I also knew it was best to wait. Wait until it was all over, and, most importantly, wait so I didn't screw up another relationship before it even began. I was very good at that.

"Sigal's alive," I said.

Her breath caught for so long that I started getting worried. "How do you know?" she asked finally.

"The guy I went to see in prison let it slip."

I told her about Malachi Razon and about the unexpected, and unexplained, connection between Sigal and Reuven.

"Do you know what Reuven's doing in Bangkok?" she asked.

I told her about Mama Dom and how she called him the *angel* of the Israelis. I had to admit that I still didn't know what she meant.

"Maybe he helps Israelis in trouble," she said.

"Maybe," I agreed. But that was extremely unlikely given the Reuven I knew, the Reuven in my past.

My cellphone rang.

"Are you alone?" I heard Aliza ask.

"No," I said, without going into details. I glanced at Reut who was bent over, massaging her toes. "But you can talk."

"Shmulik is dead," she said, letting out a primordial wail. "They found him hanging from a rope in the embassy parking garage."

I didn't respond.

"It looks like he got up on the car with the engine still running, and then pushed it out from under him with his feet. Someone went down to the garage and found him like that."

There was nothing I could say. I hadn't come here to uncover the guilty secrets of the people who crossed my path. And I'd had no intention of leaving a trail of bodies behind me. It wasn't my fault that Micha was a whore and a junkie or that Shmulik was a lonely gay. And I had no way of knowing who else was going to get hurt in the course of my investigation. I was here to find Sigal, *c'est tout*. Whatever else was going on, I didn't know, and to be honest, I didn't really care.

Aliza was alternating between gasping and moaning. "Aliza," I said in a soothing tone meant to calm her down a little. "Why did he do it?"

"Because of the pictures."

"What are you talking about? What pictures?"

"Weiss took pictures of him with young Cambodian kids and said he'd go public with them."

I could imagine what was going through her mind at the moment: What was she going to do when it all came out?

"Something wrong?" Reut asked. I motioned for her to give me another minute.

"Stay away from me," Aliza said in the voice of someone whose world was crashing down around her. "I don't know what I'm going to do, but I don't want to end up like him. I don't deserve that. And you, wherever you go, you leave scorched earth behind. I don't want to have anything more to do with you."

She disconnected. I put the phone back in my pocket.

"Shmulik, the security chief at the embassy, he committed suicide," I told Reut.

She gave me a quick look, and I could see the thoughts racing through her head. "Does it have something to do with Sigal?"

I nodded. "I don't know how, but it's all connected. Tightly connected. Everyone I've met in Bangkok is in it up to his neck."

"What about Reuven?" she asked.

"That's a good question. I guess it's time to go talk to him."

I leaned down and gave her a fluttery kiss on the brow. She smiled.

"Will you come get me later?" she asked.

"Yes," I answered. "Later."

I left without looking back. I knew that if I turned my head, I'd see her exactly as she was when I arrived, long and serene. She would stay there, stretched out on the chaise, gazing at the water and the sky and thinking about her sister, knowing that whatever happened was meant to happen and nothing could change that, not even me. She'd lie there knowing that miracles only happen when you stop being afraid.

CHAPTER TWENTY-THREE

AN EMBASSY WORKER led me to the underground parking garage, a small, cramped space with room for no more than a few cars packed close together. It was even more cramped now, teeming with local policemen and embassy security officers. I recognized Major Somnuk with his elephant ears. He turned his pockmarked face to me and gave me a sadistic smile.

"Oh, you again."

I just nodded. It didn't seem like the right moment to cement our friendship.

Shmulik's body was swaying gently from the end of a pale rope. There was something ludicrous, even comical, about the sight. His face was distorted, as if right before his death he could see the headlines when the news got out: "Chief of Security at Israeli Embassy in Bangkok Commits Suicide." The item below would read: "The body of S. was found hanging in the embassy building. The Foreign Office is working with local authorities to investigate the incident. S. had an impressive career in security."

All that was left of the mountain that was Shmulik was the hairy pot belly of a man who liked his beer, which protruded from his unbuttoned shirt. He was finally able to expose it shamelessly to the world.

Who was he thinking of when the rope began to tighten around his neck and the buzzing started behind his eyes? What was going through his head when the life began to drain out of him and the clock started counting down? I closed my eyes and tried to envision the Shmulik I once knew, when we were all still naïve, when we operated out of belief in the cause, without much self-awareness. We simply went into action and we were proud of what we were doing, no self-torment, no reservations. Again, I felt the familiar thrust of Major Somnuk's radio in my side. The bastard.

"So, Mr. Israeli investigator. A friend of yours?"

I had to give him credit. He had the intuition of a real pain in the ass.

"He was," I said.

"Was, yes," he said with a laugh. "Now he dead. Your ambassador not understand nothing. He get in my way since I come. Fucking *falang*."

He gave me another look, then peered musingly at his radio, raised his eyes, and threw me another one of those smiles I didn't like. "No need it," he said, pointing to the radio. "I not apologize for last time. I just be professional. You do same thing to me if I not respect you."

I kept quiet. Maybe, maybe not.

"We know things your ambassador not know yet," he said, gesturing toward the hanging body.

I looked him in the eye.

"We have big file on him, good pictures, too," he went on. "Your friend like to fuck little boys, especially from Cambodia. You know, they darker than us. Make them more attractive.

He know when new goods arrive. Take the youngest, or the older ones that look like children."

I let out a whistle, or maybe I just exhaled noisily. I was furious with Shmulik. A pedophile? I thought of all the years he kept his perversion a secret. Despite the myths about how people like him form communities and maintain covert contact with each other, I always suspected that their life was the very opposite of communal. They harbored a secret for most of their lives, an obsession they had to keep hidden and could never share with anyone else.

Abhorrent images took shape in my head. I could see Shmulik sitting in a bar, his eyes settling on one of the boys whose freshness shines on their faces, boys who know there will always be a horny *falang* nearby. I could see him offer the kid a drink, well aware that the young ones can't hold their liquor. He orders a Heineken for himself and a vodka and Red Bull for the boy. When it comes to drinks, they're like girls; they go for the sweet ones. The alcohol affects them quickly. After one or two drinks, they're wasted. The scene played out in my mind, and I saw the pervert hailing a cab, the boy leaning on him, and then putting his arms around him to help him in, looking left and right by force of habit. Even before the cab starts pulling away, Shmulik's hand is between the boy's legs while the kid smiles drowsily. By the time he leads him into a room, the boy is already dozing off. As Shmulik tugs off the boy's trousers, the boy mutters something, but doesn't object. The boy knows from experience that if he lies still, it will hurt less, so that's what he does.

If everything going through my head was documented in Major Somnuk's file, I thought, he had one hell of a story in his hands. The media would have a field day with it.

"What he tell you yesterday?" Somnuk asked me.

I gave him a questioning look.

"We have him under surveillance ever since we find out he had homosexual relations with Israeli that got killed," he explained.

"Isn't that against international law? He had diplomatic immunity."

The sound he emitted reminded me of a happy pig in mud. I wondered if they learned to grunt like that in Thailand's police academy.

"You friend of Khon Tom," he said. "You know better."

It was the first time he had treated me with any respect or related to my connection to a high-ranking police officer, my old friend Tom. He was right, and I knew it. But I also wondered why he had decided to mention Tom's name. Nothing happens in Bangkok without a reason.

With Shmulik's body in front of me, I didn't even want to consider the possibility that Tom was involved too. Could that be why he introduced me to Gai? So he could watch me from afar? Was it possible that he wasn't concerned for my safety, but for his own need for information? Was he keeping an eye on me in the hope I would lead him to Sigal? It seemed that everyone was caught in the web of her disappearance, a web whose dimensions I was just starting to grasp.

"You think he killed Micha Waxman?" I asked.

After photographing the scene from every angle, the crime-scene techs finally lowered Shmulik's body.

Looking me in the eye, Major Somnuk said, "Maybe. But I not think he do it himself. I think he the reason he get killed."

"Your only witness said he saw a big fat guy leaving the bar," I said.

"Yes, but then we interrogate him. After an hour, he say different. He not see anything. They tell him to say he see. You know Bangkok. You can buy anything with thousand bahts and one threat."

I looked up at the concrete ceiling beam, the only witness to the suicide. There was no sign that anything had happened here. Not even a scratch. You would have liked to leave a mark behind, wouldn't you, Shmulik? But we don't leave anything behind after we're gone. Nothing at all.

"You two close?" Major Somnuk asked.

"We used to be," I said cynically, "in another life."

That brought a genuine laugh revealing a full set of white teeth. I was afraid he was about to give me a hearty slap on the back.

"You start to understand, *falang*," he said. "That biggest compliment I ever give *falang*. Come. We leaving."

I didn't have any reason to stay there, and besides, you don't say no to a law enforcement agent in a foreign country. It's not good for the health. Ask any backpacker who ever pissed on a Mexican beach, sold posters in Japan, or did a little drug deal in India without greasing the palms of the local cops.

He took me to a small restaurant by the river where we cracked lobsters in curry sauce, slurped fresh oysters with lemon, and chomped on huge shrimp in garlic. I was beginning to think Major Somnuk and I had more in common than I had imagined. The more Mekhong whiskey was poured into the tall glasses and the less it was diluted with soda water, the closer I felt to the corrupt bastard. Closer, in fact, than I felt to anyone else around me. But I don't want to get carried away. It's not as if I were starting to like him.

"We toast our friend?" he asked. Somehow, he managed to be drunk and sober at the same time. "Now he empty, bare, open like sky. Now he scared, not know what to do, because he not ready for this moment. Western culture fucked up. No thinking about death. Just afraid. Here death is like change clothes."

What could I say? I've come face-to-face with death more than once, and I always pushed it out of my mind. I always escaped it, too.

If I'm not mistaken, at the end of the night, I hugged Somnuk, or maybe he hugged me. I can't be positive. What I do remember clearly, however, is sitting on the cool leather seat in his Mercedes and drinking from its well-stocked bar as we drove back to my hotel. I also remember that when I got out of the car with the driver, who kindly helped me to my room, I heard the major laugh. But I'm not sure what he was laughing at. Maybe at me. Or maybe at all the stupid *falangs* who stream into Bangkok thinking they've arrived in paradise and don't understand the trouble they're in for. If not right away, then at some point in the near future. Their time will come.

Because that's another name for Bangkok: Trouble in Paradise.

CHAPTER TWENTY-FOUR

I WOKE UP the next morning with an excruciating headache. It felt as if my brain were on fire. It was more than a hangover; it was the end of the world. Dozens of hammers were banging in my head, and even the slightest movement made them turn the volume up. I teetered to the shower and stood under the cold water for a few minutes. Then I wet a towel, hung it around my neck, and went back into the room where I fell onto the bed. I lay there without moving, trying merely to breathe, no more. It seemed like a huge achievement at the time. Thoughts weren't just racing through my head, they were flying through it, and not as the crow flies either. They swooped about dizzyingly as if they were at a theme park, going up on a roller coaster and then plummeting downward at terrifying speed, going round and round and round on a Ferris wheel. Within this mad rush, one thought kept re-emerging, nagging at me: Someone has been playing me the whole time.

I called Shai, my partner, back in Tel-Aviv. "Hey."

"Hey."

"How's everything there?"

"What's up?" he answered with a question.

"Other than the fact that my head's on fire?"

He didn't respond immediately, probably wondering why I chose to begin with that information. Finally, he said, "I was thinking it's about time you reported in. I haven't heard a word from you."

I remembered the early days, when we had just decided to open the agency together, S.D. International Investigations. The number of Israeli kids backpacking in the East and South America was growing, along with the number of those who blew their minds with drugs. Suddenly, they cut off all contact with home, went missing, disappeared. Their parents were worried that something had happened to them. "Let's hope this is just the beginning," we said when the first calls from frantic parents began coming in.

The hammers kept banging in my head. I didn't have the patience to play games. "Shai," I said, "I need to know how we got involved in this case."

The silence on the other end didn't last long, but my brain was on such high alert that I thought I could hear the wheels turning in his head.

"Why?" he asked.

"It's simple," I answered. "I have to know if you're playing me, too."

"I'm not," he said quietly, coldly. His tone was even colder than the towel I was now pressing to my forehead.

"Who called you about Sigal?"

"Her father, Albert Bardon. But . . ." he said, and didn't go on.

"But what?"

"Listen for yourself."

Lawsuits aren't uncommon in our business. People don't like to lose their loved ones, and when it happens, and sometimes it does, they blame everyone except for the object of the search who made the fatal mistake that cost them their life. Your son is strung out on drugs, goes tubing on the Indus River in a racing current and gets lost in the rapids? That's okay. But not finding his body is unforgiveable. That's what they paid you for, after all. So what if they've never seen a river rushing down from the Himalayas at the height of the monsoon season, uprooting rocks and tree trunks as if they were as light as feathers? So everything was documented and recorded for our own protection. It's normal procedure in our profession.

There was a pause while Shai searched for the recording of the call on the computer. I heard the familiar squeaks as he adjusted the sound and held the telephone up to the speaker so I could hear.

"Hello. My name is Albert, Albert Bardon," came the voice on the other end. He hesitated for a moment, as if he wasn't sure he'd reached the right number or how to phrase what he wanted to say. "We are concerned that something may have happened to our daughter, Sigal, in Bangkok. We haven't heard from her in several weeks. The head of security at the Israeli embassy in the city, Mr. . . ." Another pause. "I'm sorry, I don't remember his name. In any case, he advised us, unofficially, to talk to an Israeli who has lived there for a long time. Reuven Badash. We spoke to him. He recommended you. My phone number is . . ."

The dirty laundry is starting to show, I thought. Shmulik, Reuven—quite a party.

"Did you talk to Reuven?" I asked after Shai had stopped the recording.

"Yes," he admitted, without further explanation.

"And you didn't tell me?" The hammers were still going strong.

"No."

"You didn't tell me," I said, repeating furiously. "You didn't tell me!"

"I knew how you'd react to the mere mention of his name," he said. "I thought it would be better if I didn't say anything."

"You know what he's like," I said. The hammers had given way to a giant wrecking ball that was threatening to crush my head. "You know him just as well as I do. You know how he operates. He never does anything innocently. He always has an ulterior motive. And you still didn't tell me."

Shai kept silent.

"We're not like him," I said. "You saw what he was like when they kicked him out of the agency. He didn't bend an inch. So how could you, of all people, put me in a situation like this? You're my partner. You're the one person in the world I should be able to count on. You know how things ended between us."

Shai still didn't respond.

I told him that Shmulik had committed suicide. And how. Along with all the rest I'd found out about him. In revolting detail. But just the facts, no comment. He was in shock. I knew at that moment that our partnership was over. The betrayal of trust could never be healed.

"I'm having a hard time understanding what was going through your head," I said.

He took his time before answering, and finally said honestly, "What went through my head is that maybe this is more than a coincidence. Maybe Reuven is taking advantage of the opportunity to send you a message."

Now we were both silent. It was as though we were digging up everything we had buried: all the ghosts of our shared past that we had shoved into the darkest corners of our souls in the hope that we'd get through the rest of our lives without ever having to face them again. I realized that since that period in my life I'd been traveling in circles, circles that closed in on themselves and ultimately brought me to the very place I never wanted to go.

CHAPTER TWENTY-FIVE

I CALLED THE number Barbu had given me. I'd been avoiding it, but I couldn't put it off any longer. An effeminate male voice answered: "Sawadee khrup, Reuven Enterprises Incorporated."

"Can I speak to Reuven, please?"

"Reuven not here. Who calling?"

"An old friend," I said.

"Oh, from Israel?"

I was about to say something nasty when I decided to give it another minute or two to find out what I needed to know. "When will he be back?"

"He come. Be here soon."

"When?" I asked, knowing that time could have a virtual dimension in the East.

"Soon," he repeated. "Maybe hour. I not know."

I was starting to wonder what kind of operation Reuven was running and what exactly Reuven Enterprises did. I took down the address he gave me: Jasmine Hotel, Nana district.

Nana is where they sent American soldiers in the Vietnam War for R & R. But instead of rest and recuperation, they went for I & I, intercourse and intoxication. Bangkok was the ideal location, not far and relatively cheap, allowing them to

engage in their chosen activities for a few hours more before
they were flown back to Vietnam, perhaps never to return.

In the 1960s and '70s, the Jasmine Hotel attracted beat-
niks, hippies, and other misfits who shunned the establishment. They'd sit around the pool with giggling local girls,
snorting, shooting up, and making fun of the DEA agents.
Everyone knew who they were. Almost every day, a chamber-
maid would find a foreigner dead from an overdose in one of
the rooms. Back then, people indulged freely in drugs and
were indifferent to death. It was before the AIDS era. If they
got gonorrhea, they stood in line for a shot of penicillin that
made their butt numb for a day, and then went on fucking.
Sometimes they didn't even wait a day.

Nowadays, Nana attracts Arabs from the Gulf States, some
in galabias and others in Western garb and a baseball cap they
bought in the market for a buck. They prefer the fat whores,
the ones with a lot of flesh on their bones.

As I walked to the hotel, I thought of Mona Lisa. Not
Leonardo's, but the fortune teller who goes by that name. She
frequents the side streets, accosting foreigners and persuading
them to let her read their palm. To my mind, she's like a search
dog—you let it sniff an object that belonged to the person
you're looking for and it follows a scent that only it can smell.
In the course of my investigations, I've often made use of
people like her, psychics, clairvoyants, and mediums of different varieties. Most of them were nutcases and what they
called information was babble, but every now and then, they
offer me a new, unexpected perspective. Their minds are at-
tuned to different thought waves than ours and they observe
a broader spectrum. But broader often means lack of clarity
as well. Nevertheless, in my current circumstances, with no

sounding board, no one with whom I could talk things through, share information, or brainstorm, Mona Lisa seemed the most realistic option. I figured I had nothing to lose. I might as well hear what she had to say.

I asked one of the young stall holders where I could find her, and he sent me to Surya, a half-open alleyway where all the local whores get their manicures, pedicures, and foot rubs. They go there after long hours standing on a street corner or wiggling their asses on a go-go stage. They sit down, place their feet in a small plastic basin of hot scented water, and then their toes are wrapped in steaming hot towels, and they're given a manicure and pedicure that elicit groans of pleasure. They bring their clients along, too. While they're being pampered, the ubiquitous peddlers have time to show off the latest-model cellphones they carry in plastic attaché cases. If a girl is lucky, her new boyfriend will buy her a present.

Mona Lisa was sitting at the end of a row of wooden stools set out by the manicurists. It was hard to believe that thirty years ago she'd been one of Bangkok's outstanding beauties. It was well known that this petite whore was different from the others—she liked to fuck. Not surprisingly, there was an enormous demand for her services, and consequently, she burned out quickly. Then came years of drugs, emaciation, decline. But while her body grew steadily thinner, her oval face maintained its sweetness and continued to be framed by long black hair, parted in the middle. Someone once dubbed her Mona Lisa, and it stuck.

How did she become a fortune teller? Nobody knows. It's said that one day she sat down under a big ficus tree in Lumpini Park and didn't budge for a year. She just sat there, gazing at the Sodom and Gomorrah that is Bangkok. She saw the young men who arrived fresh and full of life and then lost themselves to drugs, the naïve girls waiting for a *falang* who would be their guardian angel and take them away from the brothels. She saw it all, absorbed the pain, and her brain ceased all other activity. For a whole year she sat by herself under the tree and watched. People on their way from Lumpini Park to Silom Street would pass her and say, "Mona Lisa sees things." At least, that's the story.

Now she was sitting on a bamboo stool, a small skinny woman with a wrinkled face. Her eyes were closed and her hands were resting motionless on her inner thighs. There were two more stools in front of her. One held a blue plastic basin like the ones the ladies soaked their feet in. But Mona Lisa's basin was dry. Inside was a fifty-baht note and a few coins.

"Mona Lisa," I said.

She raised her tired face, but when she opened her eyes, I could see they still had the same enigmatic expression that Leonardo had captured with his brush. I imagined the bastard must have looked at a lot of whores in his day. Florence back then must have been like Bangkok today, a place where the air was filled with the stench of lust, intercourse, and semen mixed with cooking odors emanating from hot chili and fish oil.

She had a distant look in her eyes, as if they were focused on some faraway place.

"I need your help," I said.

I wasn't sure if she saw me or heard me. I put a hundred-baht note in her basin, but even that didn't draw a response. I fished out a thousand-baht note and passed it in front of her face. She started to come awake. Her eyes followed the bill through the air and watched as I placed it on top of the first.

I took out Sigal's passport. It had been in my pocket all this time. I hadn't even showed it to Reut, hadn't even told her I had it. I kept it hidden, as if it held the key to whatever had happened to Sigal. I opened it to the photo and held it up in front of Mona Lisa's eyes.

"I'm looking for her," I said.

She took the passport from me, placed it on her bony knees with the picture facing upward, and lay her open palms on top of it.

"I know she's alive," I said.

She closed her eyes again. I thought she might have fallen asleep, but then she opened them abruptly.

"She is very afraid," she said. "Very much fear. And she is hiding."

"Where?"

Mona Lisa didn't answer immediately. She toured her inner consciousness first, and when she returned, she said, "In the beginning I see the smile of Buddha and big fish swimming around him and she is safe. Now . . ." She fell silent.

"That much I know," I said impatiently. It wasn't bad, the way she described the temple. But Sigal wasn't there anymore.

"Where is she now?" I asked.

Again, she closed her eyes. This time it felt like an eternity before she opened them. "Now I see only water. Much water. It make the picture not clear. Fear spread out like ripples in water."

There was plenty of water in Bangkok. The canals, or what they call *khlongs*, form a complex network of channels that flow into the Chao Phraya. A lot of life goes on along the canals and the river. People looking for work, former farmers who left their failing rice fields, live in the narrow spaces between the canals and the streets and under every bridge. Was she hiding in one of the infinite number of waterside shacks? It would take years to check them all out. You'd need more than one lifetime to complete the job.

"Try again," I said, tossing another purple five-hundred-baht note into the basin.

While I waited for her to open her eyes, I gazed at the old woman and envisioned her fading away. Soon, no one will need your services anymore, I thought. Everyone's hooked up to the internet these days, expecting to find all the answers there. It won't be long before no one even remembers who you were.

This time when she opened her eyes, they seemed clearer, the way they used to look. "I see Chao Phraya. People get out of black cars and taxis. They come and go. When they come, they tense; when they go, they laugh. I see girls. They smile, they invite. Water all around. She in middle. Shaking. Maybe she cold, maybe too much drugs. Shaking. Not move from fear." She paused for a moment and then went on. "Not much time. You must find her." She rested her hands on her thighs, resuming the position she had been in when I arrived, and closed her eyes. The reading was over.

CHAPTER TWENTY-SIX

THE GROUND FLOOR of the Jasmine Hotel was occupied by a row of shops and offices that opened onto the street and sported signs in every color, shape, and language. One in pink read, "Ravi, Your Tailor in Bangkok," the message spelled out in English, Thai, and Hindi; above a Lebanese shawarma restaurant was a green sign reading "Little Beirut" in English, Thai, and Arabic, with a crescent below. On another sign, written only in English, were the words "Reuven Enterprises Inc." One of those names that doesn't give anything away.

I pushed on the glass door. Inside was a human zoo representing every stage in some weird evolution. In the background, the whiny disco music that only Thai people can tolerate was playing. The office was a busy hive of *kathoey*, ladyboys, the young men who come to Bangkok in droves looking to earn the twelve hundred dollars they need for a sex change operation by working in the sex industry or in cosmetic and hair salons. Peeling the banana, the boys—or is it girls?—call the removal of their penis.

Kathoeys were going in and out. The one at the reception desk near the door was a prime example, having undoubtedly undergone every surgical procedure possible. She raised heavily made-up eyes with long artificial lashes and flashed me a smile with her deep red lips. "Yes?" she asked.

I told her I was looking for Reuven.

"Reuven no yet come."

With such excellent English she could go far, I thought cynically.

I sank into a faux leather armchair nearby and picked up one of the glossy fashion magazines piled on the low table beside me. I leafed through it, but I didn't actually read it. Across from me, a long row of *kathoeys* sat in front of huge mirrors applying layers of makeup. Others went upstairs to the dressing room and came back down to show themselves off to their friends. The word that rang out again and again, beginning nearly every sentence, was *tai*, the local pronunciation of "die," as in "to die for," or in *tai di chun*, "I'm dying."

Tai di chun, my makeup doesn't look good. Every *falang* fool will see right away that I'm a man without having to check under my skirt.

Tai di chun, the damn silicon. One of my breasts is sliding down.

Tai di chun, my pubic hair is showing in the crotch of my body suit.

So many reasons to die, and all with a magnitude of emotion and intensity that no foreigner can understand.

They completely ignored me. I was watching them so intently that I didn't even notice the man who came in a few minutes after me. But so many of the *kathoeys* hurried over to him, kissing him on the cheek and making a slight curtsy as they held their hands in the *wai* gesture, that eventually I became aware of his presence.

He was standing with his back to me. The shudder that ran through my body said it all. Then he turned and looked at me. His hair was dyed black and the skin on his face was stretched tight from repeated Botox injections, but there was no mistaking the eyes. It was him. There might have been a few artificial improvements, but it was still him.

I stood up. The moment our eyes met, the many years since I'd last seen him evaporated and everything came flooding back. I was overwhelmed by the rage I'd carried with me all this time, the kind of rage you can only feel toward someone you once loved.

"You finally came," Reuven said. "It took you years." His face didn't move when he spoke. It was as if the voice emerged from a mask.

"So now we're face-to-face," I heard myself say drily. Reuven had betrayed me. It was an unforgiveable betrayal, the worst kind. The betrayal of a brother. And now he had gotten me tangled up in some mess again. I just didn't know what kind of mess.

"Yes," he answered. "Look how far we had to go to meet up again in this hellhole."

He noticed me scrutinizing his face, searching. "They didn't cover the scar," he said. "I couldn't let go of it." He turned his cheek toward me, showing me where the terrorist had stabbed him before I took the shithead out. That was a long time ago, when we were young, and someone first got the idea of having us disguise ourselves as Arabs in order to work undercover in the territories.

Reuven extended his hand. "Isn't it time for us to shake?" I reached for it. You can't change a handshake. You remember

it, your hand remembers it. Reuven's was always exceptionally firm.

"Can I have my hand back?" I said when he continued to
hold onto it.

"You're still mad at me," he stated.

"Very perceptive of you," I said.

"I didn't expect you to forgive me, but I did expect you to
move on."

"Sorry to disappoint you."

Reuven walked toward the only seating area in the room
that wasn't covered in articles of clothing, overflowing ashtrays, and spray cans in vivid shades of pink, blue, and red. He
motioned to a chair. I remained standing.

"Come on, sit down," he said. "We have a lot to talk about."

We sat down beside a glass table with iron legs in the shape
of naked women. On it was a bottle of Suntory Japanese
whiskey and two frosted glasses. Reuven poured us each a shot
of whiskey.

"Neat or Thai style?" he asked.

"Neat."

We didn't clink glasses, merely drank in silence. I'd hardly
taken a sip before he was already pouring himself another generous shot, which he proceeded to belt down as if he was in
need of hydration.

I looked around the large room. From where I was sitting
before, it seemed to be buzzing with life. From here it looked
like I was in a theater watching a performance that would be
over in an hour.

"Do you know why I brought you here?" he asked abruptly.

"Brought me?"

"Brought you—set the wheels in motion. What difference does it make? You think it was random chance that made you come to Bangkok at this particular moment in time? Nothing random about it. Everyone follows their own karma. To the letter. Initially, I thought you were the only one who could handle the investigation and save my sorry ass. I figured I could work the rest out on my own after that. Then I realized that by the time you got here, it would be too late. But still, I wanted you to be here at the end. Nobody else, just you."

"So in a nutshell, you got me in deep shit once, and now you're doing it again," I said.

"That's one way of looking at it, but it's not what I wanted. I know it's hard for you to believe me."

"You still think I owe you," I said. "You screw up again so you bring me here as a last resort and then you drag me down with you into your fucked-up life."

"I expected it to end differently," he said. "I know now I was too optimistic."

He refilled our glasses. I was fine with that. The simplest way for me to understand what had happened, what was happening at the moment, was to let him keep drinking and keep talking.

"When I first came to Bangkok," he related, "I was caught up in the freedom here, like a lot of foreigners. No accountability, not for anything, not to anyone. Just as long as you don't step on anyone's toes, you can do what you want. As they say here, it's all *mai pen rai*—doesn't matter. Right away I know it's a place where I can put my old life behind me and start a new one. At that point, you're more in touch with yourself than you've ever been before. You learn the truth about yourself, even if it's not so pretty."

I knew exactly what he meant. It went even deeper than that. And I knew it was pure luck that he was telling this story and not me. We could easily have traded places.

"In the first few months, I burned through everything I had in a whirlwind of excitement, drugs, and sex. *Mai pen rai* if you sleep with three girls as long as you pay the bar bill, the hotel, and the ladies themselves. *Mai pen rai* if you shoot up heroin. *Mai pen rai* whatever you do to forget your shitty past. I tried. I feasted on every kind of fuck and drug there is. I earned myself the reputation of a freak even in the depraved world of Bangkok.

"Then one day, the well dried up. I'd cashed in everything I had, my pension plan, my savings, my life insurance. It's all gone. Not a penny left. After a week or two of living on soup and handouts from friends, or rather *former* friends, I pick up the last thing I still possess, my camera, and start taking pictures in Patpong.

"By now I know the place inside and out. I photographed the girls obsessively, just like I fucked them. The young girls forced to become women, the ones who become mothers. I shot what was left of their innocence after years of shoving ping pong balls and razor blades into their cunts, along with the dicks of crazy Chinamen, drunken Russians, potbellied Germans, and noisy Israelis. After a wild ride taking pictures of Bangkok's sewers, I put together a calendar of Patpong girls that sells like hot cakes. Who wouldn't buy it? It's a collection of everything a lonely white man ever fantasized about.

"Then I open this agency for *kathoey* models, but I'm still hanging out and shooting pictures in Patpong, Nana, and Soi Cowboy, the only places I can find someone to pretend to care about me. Places where I can forget. I spend a few years like that, but every time I look in the mirror all I see is hollowness. I'm dying inside.

"One day some cops come up to me on Khao San and say an Israeli kid is walking around in his birthday suit, going up to people and challenging them to a war of who can keep from cracking a smile longest. If they don't want to play his game, he spits at them. They don't know what to do with him. He doesn't have a penny on him, so there's no point in arresting him. But if someone doesn't get him out of there, they won't have any choice. They'll be forced to pick him up, and I know they'll beat him to a pulp.

"I take him home with me. What else can I do? He's Israeli, and all of a sudden that means a lot to me. It's as if I have another chance to give without expecting anything in return. I keep him tied to a chair for four days until he gets clean. He screams incessantly. Now and then he sobers up a little and asks for water and then he pisses and says all the fluids are draining out of him and starts screaming again.

"I manage to locate his parents. I still have a few connections. His father gets on the first plane and takes him home, straight into a psychiatric ward. There are other incidents after that. In Khao San they learn that if an Israeli loses it, and that happens every couple of days, it's better to call Reuven than the Tourist Police."

I continued to sit in silence. We'd almost finished the bottle, or more precisely, Reuven had.

"One day I get a call from a guesthouse in Khao San. They tell me they have an Israeli girl who passed out a few hours ago and they can't wake her up. They think she OD'd. They want me to come get her. If she dies in the guesthouse, they'll lose their license. When I get there, I find the most amazing Israeli woman I've ever seen. She's spectacular. It's love at first sight."

Reuven paused for a moment before going on.

"Sigal was beautiful even lying half-dressed on a cot, as white as a ghost. One of her legs was hanging off the bed and her arms were limp and lifeless. But beautiful. Incredibly beautiful.

"I take her home, give her a shot of Valium every six hours to reduce her body's craving for heroin. For two days I sit vigil over her, day and night. I've never seen anyone like her. She's got the softness and peacefulness I've always searched for and could never find in myself.

"On the third morning she opens her eyes, gazes at me, and says, 'I was having a nightmare and you were like a light in the darkness.' Then she smiles. If I could only freeze that moment. But nothing stays the same in this world. Everything changes.

"The next two weeks are a marathon of wild lovemaking. We found each other, physically and emotionally, like soul mates. We lie in bed for hours with her head on my chest, not talking, just staring at the ceiling. Once I ask her what she's thinking about and she says 'nothing.' She says she kicked the habit. Thinking is a waste of time.

"One morning she disappears. Two days later, I get a call from another guesthouse. She's lying in her own puke beside a bucket of needles and speed and every other kind of junk you can shove into your body. When she sobers up this time, she tells me how sorry she is. We both like to live on the edge, she says. Then she's my incredible lover again, and she has so much love to give.

"But the story just repeats itself. She disappears, I find her. The third time she's lying wasted in a Chinese hotel outside

Bangkok. She's selling herself for drug money. Fucked a whole tourist bus. When I get there, they're still in the lobby, tying their overstuffed suitcases with rope so they don't burst open. They bought up half the markets in Bangkok. And they're showing each other the pictures they took with their new digital cameras. I know exactly what's in them. The Chinese kiss and tell.

"I know I have to do something fast or I'll lose her forever. We can't keep on the way we are. I love her, but even if I sell everything I have, borrow from everyone I know, I won't have enough to start a new life with Sigal somewhere far from anything that reminds us of Bangkok or Israel."

Reuven fell silent, scanning my face for a reaction.

"So you arrange for her to work as a mule," I said. "You know she'll do anything to get money, if not for you, then for drugs."

"I sent her to Weiss," Reuven acknowledged. "He needed someone to transport a large shipment of heroin to southern Thailand. From there it would go on to Malaysia or Singapore. I have no idea who the buyer was. I didn't ask questions."

"The *angel* of Bangkok," I said sarcastically.

There was a pause before he went on. "I did the math. She'd be paid well to smuggle the package to the south. But that isn't enough for me. It always amazes me that kids from good homes are willing to take a huge risk for a few thousand dollars. It's a fatal mistake, and they pay a heavy price for it, destroying themselves and their families. They rot in the worst prisons in the third world, waiting years for a trial and forking out tens of thousands of dollars on attorneys and bribes just to survive. Naïve kids in a foreign prison."

"So you decide to cash in on the package," I said.

He nodded. "I know I won't have any trouble selling it to Weiss's competitors. Even if they only pay me half of what it's worth, it'll still be enough for us to disappear and start over in one of the cheap, less-traveled, places in Central America. An island in Honduras, somewhere on the coast of Guatemala. A place where I can buy a piece of beach with palm trees, where you don't see a soul for miles, except for crows and parrots and water fowl. Maybe a fisherman from time to time. A place where no one asks how much cash you brought with you."

"What went wrong?" I asked.

"I waited for her on the train going south. She didn't show up. I didn't take into account that the drugs had fucked with her mind. She didn't give a damn about the future. The only thing that mattered to her was her next fix."

"And you didn't anticipate that?"

"No," he answered. For the first time, I heard the anguish in his voice. "All I could see were the wonderful years ahead of us. She was my redemption, my only, probably my last, chance at a real life. I was blind."

"How did she know Micha Waxman?"

"He was a shadow, the kind that sticks to you. Now and then he worked as a mule, an errand boy. I guess he heard about the shipment and found out that Sigal was going to carry it."

"I found her things in his room," I said.

"I know. I was there. I took his passport." I saw the hint of a smile and for a moment he was the Reuven I once knew, a master of dirty tricks. Then the inscrutable mask was back in place. "There's a gap I can't fill," he continued. "A few hours, maybe a day or two, when everything went haywire. I don't know what happened during that time."

"Who killed Micha?"

He sat in silence for a long time. Finally, he said, "Weiss, naturally. If he didn't do it himself, he sent one of his minions."

"Micha was a little fish. He was taking a big risk by killing him."

"For him, Micha was a gnat, an annoying little mosquito you can squash in your hand. He probably found out that he was with Sigal after she got the package and thought he could tell him where she was hiding."

"How would Weiss find out something like that?"

"From our friend, Shmulik," Reuven said bitterly. "He sold him out for a bunch of fresh Cambodian kids."

"So we're left with Weiss. And you think he'll just write it off? Twenty-one K of heroin?"

"No." He attempted a smile, but it looked more like a grimace. "You get it now? You're the only person I could turn to. But I couldn't simply call you out of the blue and say, 'Dotan, I need your help.'"

"I would've told you go fuck yourself," I said.

"I know."

It was time. I took out Sigal's passport, the document that had been sitting quietly in my pocket all this time, not budging except for a brief sortie into the hands of Mona Lisa. "I have her passport," I said.

Without a word, he reached out his hand.

I placed it on his open palm.

With a shaking hand, he opened the blue cover embossed with a gold menorah. "Once upon a time this meant the world to us," he said, raising his eyes to look at me. "You remember when we got our first passports? The first time we went overseas?"

For a moment, the wall between us came tumbling down. We were joined together again, like so long ago. A holiday trip to Greece, our first vacation after graduation from the academy, just before we undertook what we believed would be a lifelong commitment. The naiveté of youth. We landed in Athens. The first night, one of us got plastered on local retsina wine, and the other picked up an American girl and spent the night with her on the roof of our hotel opposite the Acropolis. We told the story so many times that I can't remember any more which of us did what, who got drunk and who got laid.

Reuven leafed through the passport and then stared at the picture for a long time. "It's a lousy photo," he said as he returned it to me. "You hold on to it. I think it's too late for it to be any use to me."

CHAPTER TWENTY-SEVEN

IVAN THE DURIAN stormed in through the open door to the street, accompanied by two armed Thai gorillas. He moved agilely, despite his size and the added weight of what looked like a recoilless rifle. Whatever it was, it looked very persuasive.

Weiss appeared right behind them, looking right and left as if he was surprised there was no one there to usher him in. He crossed the room with measured steps and sat down in the armchair beside me. He seemed to have dressed for a night out—tight custom-made suit, loud silk tie, white snakeskin boots. I wondered how he survived the heat in that outfit.

Ivan motioned to one of his goons, who pulled a plastic bag out of his pocket and squeezed it until it popped, making a sound like a gunshot. Extracting a chilled wet towel, he handed it to Weiss.

"Can't your fucking fish sauce do anything quietly?" he complained.

"*Izvini*—sorry, boss," Ivan apologized.

Weiss wiped his face and then passed the towel over his neck and arms. "Hot outside," he said.

We sat in silence.

"Having fun?" He surveyed the room until his eyes were caught by a *kathoey* who was making a conspicuous effort to go about her business as if nothing was happening. "This your thing?" he asked Reuven with visible repulsion. "Disgusting. I don't mind sticking it in an ass now and then, if I finish off a bottle of vodka and do some speed first. But them? All synthetic. Yech."

Another glance at the firepower his muscle was wielding was enough to convince me to keep quiet. There wasn't much I could do in any case. So I just sat there wondering what this circus looked like from the sidelines.

Weiss fidgeted in his chair, threw one leg over the armrest, and then replaced it on the floor. He was clearly uncomfortable. However, he arranged himself in the low chair, the tight suit pinched. Finally, he turned to Reuven. "I can't figure you out. You trying to get happy at my expense? You know if you're happy, I suffer. What kind of karma is that?"

Reuven didn't respond.

"Do you think I don't suffer enough?" Weiss went on. "Is that why you're trying to hurt me? Tell me where Sigal is and where the package is and I'll make it quick."

Reuven still didn't say a word.

"You think I'm an idiot?" Weiss was speaking in a low voice, but the blood was already rising in his face. "What? You have contempt for me? For where I come from? You don't like my accent? What? You think if you don't talk to me, I'm not here?"

Silence.

"Do you know?" Weiss asked me.

The goon loudly popped another bag and handed Weiss a fresh wet towel. Weiss threw Ivan a nasty look.

"*Izvini*—sorry, boss," Ivan said again.

"*Verblud*—motherfucker," Weiss said before turning back to us. "You want the truth? I'm sick and tired of the whole thing. I'm just trying to run a business. Lots of loony Israelis show up on my doorstep wanting to make a killing. 'Weiss, what should I invest in? I trust you. Tell me what to do.' I open my door to them, show them a good time, give them a bottle of my best vodka, send them my best whores. Best of the best. And then what? They meet another fucking Israeli who says, 'What're you doing? You're crazy to trust that Russian. He's screwing with you.' They hear that and they say, 'Really? That's how it is?' and they change their mind. They don't understand that the other guy already changed their life. The next day they're in prison awaiting trial and their life isn't worth a dime. So whattaya say?"

We continued to invoke our right to remain silent.

"A weaker man wouldn't be able to make any sense of it," Weiss went on. "It would drive him crazy. But me? I say it's all karma. They come, they go, it doesn't make any difference to me. Just don't shit on Weiss."

We kept our thoughts to ourselves.

"But then there's the exception. You get what I'm saying?"

Ivan was still leaning on the wall next to the table. His goons were standing, feet apart, pointing their guns at us. Weiss kept up his spiel. "Law of probability," he said. "It also works for karma. It says there's always an exception to the rule."

Nice, I thought. Even the Russian gangster reflects on the meaning of life in his spare time. This must be an enlightened era. Except that I didn't know if we were part of his spare time or his business hours. I was becoming increasingly concerned by the way the "conversation" was going, but there was nothing

I could do about it. So I just sat there, sinking deeper into my chair.

Weiss stood up, straightened his clothes, and began pacing back and forth between Reuven and me.

"What does the exception do? It fucks everyone. It screws with everyone's life. What? People don't know how to enjoy life anymore. They can't live and let live?"

I sank even deeper in my chair. I could imagine what was about to happen.

"You want the truth? I'm sick and tired of the whole thing," Weiss repeated. "I don't care about the package, I don't care about the money. I just want to be through with it. I can't understand why it's taking so long. Everyone in Bangkok knows the story. They're waiting to see how it ends, what Weiss is gonna do."

He paused and turned to me. "You know what this is doing to my reputation?"

I shook my head.

"My name is mud," he said. "I see it in their eyes. They're laughing at me. They're saying Weiss lost his touch. Got soft, like an oyster. The only oysters I want are for lunch. On a plate."

He continued pacing, and then stopped in front of Reuven. "So I'm ending it here and now."

Without warning, he drew a small pistol from the pocket of his custom-made suit. Before I could jump on him, the two goons leapt at me and held my arms down. Weiss fired. Three shots. One—two—three.

Reuven folded up in his chair, his head hitting the glass table and throwing the Buddha onto the floor as he fell. His flowery shirt was stained by the blood rushing from his chest.

Weiss gave the signal, and Ivan and his goons vanished out of sight. As he walked to the door, he turned and said, "At the end, a man is nothing. Dust. But he was less than nothing." He marched out, but not before spitting on the floor.

The room filled with the frantic screams of the *kathoeys*. I went over to Reuven. He was lying on the floor, breathing heavily, his eyes open. Foam and blood issued from his mouth. With difficulty, he focused his eyes on me. "All..." Every word required a supreme effort. "All the signs were there. They always are," he mumbled, struggling for breath. "Don't go."

Nodding, I took his hand. Once again, I was pulling him forward, like the time I made him finish the climb up the mountain when there wasn't an ounce of strength left in his body. But back then the hand I grabbed was strong and sweaty. This time it was limp and cold. Nevertheless, it was still Reuven's hand, just as I remembered it. Holding it, I again felt the bond we had once had. But most of all, I felt an overwhelming compassion for him that I couldn't explain.

His eyes closed.

"Reuven," I begged, "stay with me."

Making an enormous effort, he opened his eyes, and with what might have been the trace of a smile, he whispered, "I screwed up. I always screw up, don't I?"

The light was draining from his eyes. Again, he struggled to open them, gasping for breath. "Can I count on you? Like I used to?"

I remained silent, merely squeezing his hand gently. With the last of his strength, he strained to make himself understood. "Naor, you have to find Sigal. Release her from her torment. Live up to your reputation."

I saw him sinking, his senses fading one after the other, until his eyes lost their grasp on my face. I closed the lids gently and placed my hands over them. He stopped breathing. It was the first time I had ever seen him at peace.

He had to wait for me to show up before he could die, I thought. It was a very long wait.

CHAPTER TWENTY-EIGHT

MY CELLPHONE RANG. Tom.

"She's at Chao Phraya Body Massage," he informed me.

"And you've known this the whole time?"

"Not the whole time," he answered. I waited while he coughed from the perennial cigarette between his lips. "I've known for a while, but I couldn't tell you. You know us Thais. We're superstitious. I believed if I said anything, you wouldn't go where your fate was meant to take you. All things must be said and done at the right time. No shortcuts. That's the real meaning of karma."

"You could have saved a few people from ending up as bodies in the river," I said.

Tom laughed. "I doubt it. Anyway, I'm nothing compared to a shipment of drugs. It can seal a lot more fates than I can."

You can't change the mentality of a Thai Buddhist, I thought. Not even if you send him to Princeton. What mattered now was that my karma had finally led me to Sigal.

"Gai will be waiting for you there. Chao Phraya Body Massage in Pratunam. The cab drivers know it." I thought he'd disconnected, but then I heard him add quietly, "I'll make sure Weiss stays out of the way."

I consider anything Tom says as sacred. Well, maybe not sacred like the sayings of Buddha, but there have always been two gods in Bangkok: Buddha and whoever is pulling the strings. That's why the city is like paradise—it's a beautiful place, but danger is always lurking.

I called Reut and told her to be ready in half an hour. I was coming to pick her up.

When I arrived at her hotel, she was waiting in the lobby. She was everything I had always wanted. She had on the same summery dress she was wearing the first time I saw her, and her eyes were hidden behind large whimsical white sunglasses that made me smile. I could tell she had chosen them deliberately for that purpose, even though she herself wasn't smiling. I felt her anxiety and distress.

The cab let us off in the parking lot of the massage parlor that bore the name of Bangkok's river. It wasn't very busy in these early afternoon hours. A cab stopped to let out a customer, while another cab came by to pick up a man leaving the establishment.

Gai was waiting just inside the door. "Come," he said.

We passed a large window. A row of girls in bikinis with number tags were sitting behind it. They followed us closely with their eyes, anxious to see how the story would play out. News travels fast through the sewers of Bangkok. Next, we passed the cashier. The man behind the counter scrutinized us, but didn't say a word. We climbed a wide flight of stairs to the rooms on the second floor. Most of the doors were open, the rooms not in use. A few cleaning women were hard at work. I saw the large tubs, the thick mattresses on the floor, and all the accoutrements needed to grant a customer a fleeting moment of pleasure.

Gai took out a key and unlocked a door. Inside, on a large waterbed, Sigal was lying like a limp rag, her body trembling. A barefoot girl in shorts and a tank top dipped a cloth in a bucket of ice water and gently wiped her forehead.

Sigal opened her eyes when we walked in, as if she had been waiting for us. "Reut, you're here, you came. Take me home," she said. Her breaths were short and shallow. She was struggling to get enough air into her lungs, almost choking, but her face was animated.

I called Tom. "I need one last favor from you," I said, explaining the situation. As usual, when a swift response is required, Tom has the magic touch that makes things happen. Ten minutes later, a doctor was there. He examined Sigal, gave her a series of shots, and hooked her up to an IV. "Her condition is critical," he pronounced. "She's got a severe liver infection. It's lucky I got here in time. Let her rest for a couple of hours. You can move her tonight."

For the next few hours we sat by her bed, not exchanging a word. The one time I went out to have a smoke, I found Gai standing by the door. He must have been there all this time.

When Sigal opened her eyes, it was getting dark and the neon lights were coming on outside. Reut leaned over her. "How are you feeling?" she asked softly. Sigal reached her hand out to her sister. It was weak, gaunt, and pale. "Take me away from here," she said.

Reut raised her eyes. They were still bright green, but I could see a shadow of apprehension pass over them.

I nodded as convincingly as I could: don't worry.

CHAPTER TWENTY-NINE

WITH ONE CALL to El Al's operations manager in Bangkok, I arranged for Sigal and Reut to be on the plane to Tel Aviv that night. An ambulance took her onto the runway, and an airport worker pushed the stretcher the rest of the way while Reut walked beside it holding her sister's hand.

"I'm sorry," Sigal said.

"Me, too," Reut answered. "I can't tell you how sorry I am."

Sigal began weeping. Reut leaned down and kissed her gently on the cheek, brushing away the tears.

I thought of Reuven lying on the floor, blood flowing from his fatal wounds; I thought of Shmulik who didn't leave a single mark on the concrete beam; of Yair Shemesh—Barbu, who I'd never see again. Sigal's weeping had been replaced by moans. Reut stroked her, whispering words of comfort. For my part, I made an attempt to remain indifferent. It was one of those moments when everything's over and you feel empty. It's not the time for soul-searching yet, I told myself. That time will come.

There was only one more question I had to ask. "Sigal, where's the duffel bag?"

With an effort, she turned her head to me. "You'll believe me, right?"

"I'll try," I answered.

"When I got to the train station, I saw Weiss's men and I panicked. I knew I had to get away. I couldn't find Micha. He was with me up to then, but suddenly he was gone. I was terrified. I shoved the bag into a locker, took the key, and ran. I hung the key on a ribbon around my neck, but it felt like it was burning me. I hid in Wat Arun. One day I was standing by the river watching the catfish, and without thinking I took it off and threw it in the water. It was swallowed by a fish."

I was about to ask her the number of the locker, but then I thought of Weiss and Valium. I laughed. "Those catfish must be very happy," I said. All of a sudden, I remembered the Buddha amulet I'd been wearing all this time. On impulse, I took it off and placed it in Sigal's hand.

"It's from Reuven," I said. So what if I was lying and it was from the cabdriver. "I think it has the power to make sure things come out right in the end, like they're supposed to, like they were supposed to from the beginning."

The stretcher was carried onto the plane. Reut gave me a long look, but didn't say anything. My cellphone rang. I debated whether to answer it.

I accepted the call. Another mistake. The type of mistake I should already have learned not to make.

It was Shai. The schmuck, I thought. He calls me as if nothing happened. But I guess he knows me better than I know myself. After all, here I was answering his call, and my adrenaline was already flowing.

"Dotan," he said, "we have another case. India this time. There's no point in coming back here. Catch a flight to Delhi.

I'm sending you the details. Get in touch with Colonel Krishna. He knows you're coming. He's already started gathering intel."

"You always drown me in info," I complained sarcastically.

"It's just coming in now. The situation isn't clear yet. All I know for sure is that some Israeli kid went on retreat to an ashram in the north and disappeared into thin air."

I disconnected. Reut was still gazing at me. I gave her an innocent look in return.

"You're not coming back with me?" she asked.

"No."

"Okay, I'm a patient woman. As long as there's hope. Just be careful not to start using words like baby or sweetie. I've heard them enough."

I didn't respond. To be honest, I was in shock. I have to change my style, that's for sure, I thought.

"Why are you looking at me like that?" she asked. "Don't you know I'll be waiting for you? Men don't understand anything."

She was already standing on the first step. From above, the flight attendant motioned for her to hurry up, they wanted to close the doors. She turned back to me and crouched down. "Kiss me," she said.

It was the kiss of life.